WHO SAILS WITH DRAKE, SAILS WITH ADVENTURE!

Set amidst the swirling tide of intrigue and politics of Elizabethan England is this gripping novel of a dashing young swordsman, Talbot Slanning.

Having been involved in a duel that ended in death, Talbot's fast blade earned him not glory but flight—and his rescuer was the pirate Francis Drake. It was sail for the New World to plunder its gold—or stay in England and hang.

But what he found refuge among turned out to be a forest of Spanish blades, and Talbot had only his quick wit and his thrusting wrist to keep him on the road to a buccaneer's fortune.

DONALD BARR CHIDSEY has made an enviable name for himself both as a writer of excellent historical novels, including such as *Captain Crossbones* and *The Pipes are Calling*, and also as a writer of historical biographies, including those of Sir Walter Raleigh, Marlborough, and Bonnie Prince Charlie.

His own life has been as full of adventure as his writings. He has covered a good part of the earth in tramp steamers, pearl shell boats, and private yachts. He has lived in the South Seas, has been a newspaperman, actor, farmer, road gang foreman, mountaineer, boxer and fencer. During the war he served with the British, New Zealanders, Highlanders, the Free French, and the United States Army.

At the present time he lives quietly in Lyme, Connecticut, and seems content to confine further adventures to the pen.

Buccaneer's Blade

by Donald Barr Chidsey

WILDSIDE PRESS

CHAPTER ONE

Talbot threw crabs for the third time, and made a refusing motion.

"No use, Robin. The dice just won't grin at me. Pick up your money."

He yanked gloves from his sword-belt.

"I've lingered too long already. I'll be riding half the night."

"Aye, the second half," said Robert Butterwalk. "But the first half, I'll warrant, will be spent under Abergavenny's roof."

He shook his large head, and there was worry in his eyes. He was fond of his friend Talbot, and proud of him. They had hunted together as boys. Robert Butterwalk still hunted but now he was growing fat. Talbot Slanning, very grand in his new clothes, had recently made a tour of the Continent. This tour was interrupted by the news from home that he had become an orphan and at the same time a pauper. He'd had to borrow money to get back. And now Talbot Slanning was a gentleman in the household of the Earl of Sussex. It was not infrequently that he galloped through the West Country on his master's business, a penniless young man, but a gay one. To Robert Butterwalk, the stay-at-home, he was a drop splashed from the distant fabulous rainbowed court when as today he drew rein in Chagford for a beaker of sack and a half-hour at hazard. And since he couldn't afford it, he had of course lost.

"I don't like it," Robert said.

When Robert was worried he was worried all over, just as when he was happy he laughed from hair to feet.

"D'ye think Katherine will lure me to my ruin, eh?"

"Gillard," Robert muttered, shaking his head.

"He's still about?" Talbot frowned.

"Aye. He has a shallop at Dartmouth. Says it trades with the Low Countries, but it's the opinion of all men hereabout that it's nothing more nor less than a pirate ship."

"Likely."

"'Tis called *Gillard's Pride*. But Tom's not in it much. He's here in Chagford half the time, and when he's here he's mostly at Abergavenny Manor."

"Pirate or no, he wastes his time there. Kate'll have none of him." Talbot lowered his voice to a confidential tone.

"Aye, and that's just what troubles me. Gillard's a man who dislikes opposition. He rides it down. He crushes it. He and his bullies—"

"Buggar him and his bullies! There's such a thing as law in this country!"

"Not the part of it that Tom Gillard controls. This part here. Besides the bullies, he's got cousins as thick as raisins in a cake, and every man-jack of 'em glittering bright in some particular corner of the court. Eh, why they tell me that Sir Francis Monckton himself is a cousin of Gillard's and is to stay with him here this very night. How can you buck a man like that?"

"I care not for Frank Monckton," Talbot muttered.

"But the Queen does."

Yes. Talbot knew, none better, the influence that suave dandy exercised over Elizabeth Tudor. Everybody knew it. Leicester himself trembled at the thought, even though, nominally at least, Monckton was a member of Leicester's own party. So Monckton and Tom Gillard were kin? Talbot sniffed his disdain; but he didn't like it.

Robert Butterwalk picked up the money. He chuckled cynically.

"Gillard was here last night, late. I think he'd come from courting Kate, though he'd not admit it. He was as black as a thundercloud. Threw some coins on the table and called for dice."

"And you bettered him?" Talbot asked, amazed.

"Twenty-two harrynobles. I made four straight passes. And then I wagered the whole pile against the pistol he carried. Here it is—a beauty, eh?"

Talbot eyed this weapon with interest, though also with no little repugnance. It was Italian, a blue steel barrel about eighteen inches long, resting on carved Circassian walnut. The huge fishtail butt was made of bone and ivory.

"You should never carry a thing like that with you," he said. "It's dangerous!"

"Aye, but it's beautiful, too."

He fondled the weapon proudly and tenderly.

"Dangerous," Talbot repeated. "They ought to forbid that sort of thing."

He pulled on his guantlets. He slapped his friend's shoulder.

"Well, I'm away. Don't eat too much of that junket and cream, Robin, or the next time I see you, you'll be as fat as a Herefordshire sow."

"Ho, I'm that already!"

It was wonderful to be in Chagford again, Talbot re-

7

flected as he strolled out of the inn. It was good to smell the honeysuckle, to see the tall hedgethorns, to smile at old familiar faces, and to cast at hazard with Robin Butterwalk, even though he lost, and to call a greeting to Tim the hostler. Talbot never had a serious thought of returning to Chagford and spending the rest of his life there, like Robert, hunting, guzzling cider, bowling on the green through long sunlit afternoons. No, the city was his place—the larger, livelier world, the swirl of war and politics, the court, the glitter of great people around the greatest brightest glitter of them all, the Queen. He had been seven years away from Devonshire, and it was now just a blurred but pleasant memory to him. Except when, as today, he passed through on an errand for his master and paused at Chagford to exchange greetings and to visit Katherine Abergavenny.

Chiefly to visit Katherine. In the Earl's household it was understood that young Slanning should be sent into the West Country as often as this could conveniently be arranged; and Sussex himself never gave him such a mission without a sly smile and a wink at those who stood nearby. Oh, it was well enough known, in London as in Chagford, where Talbot Slanning's heart inclined! But he did not care. He'd shout it from the housetops. He was very happy today.

He was a shade less happy when he stepped out into the highroad and met Thomas Gillard of Gillard's Elm.

"Ho! Business brings thee here, Slanning?"

Talbot bridled at the "thee," as no doubt he was meant to do. It was a word applied only to very close relatives, or sweethearts—or servants. Its use of anyone else could be called a direct challenge, like giving the lie or slapping the face. Many a man had lugged out his sword as in rage he cried: "Don't you 'thou' me!"

Talbot chose to ignore it, though he did so with difficulty. He didn't like Tom Gillard, never had.

The man was huge. He had only just dismounted and was approaching the door of the Three Crowns, intent upon refreshment. But now he paused, as he spoke to Talbot Slannings. Beside Slanning, who was slim and of normal height Tomas Gillard loomed enormous. Not fat, either. There wasn't an ounce of fat on him. His hair was naturally dark, and there was a great deal of it. His face had been darkened by weather. His hands were big, his neck and wrists thick; and his legs were bulging masses of muscle.

He was wearing a leather doublet, a blue velvet cape slashed with silver, a rose in his blue velvet bonnet. Yet for all this gay attire his face was grim, his brow squeezed low. He was a man eternally truculent, forever prepared to cut or thrust or if need be to punch, scratch, kick or bite. His eyes, which were small, were a very dark blue, in some lights an angry dark purple. His mouth was long and unmercifully straight, a mouth that never knew a smile. His beard, bleached an irregular yellow by the sun, was hard, stiff, coarse. There were gold rings in his ears.

"Riding to London?"

"If the lord of these parts gives me his gracious permission to do so."

"Riding *direct* to London?"

"Perhaps."

Gillard edged a little closer, moving with tiny, almost imperceptible steps. For all his size, he could be as light as a cat, and just as quick.

"*Perhaps*, eh? Look here, Slanning, 'twould be well if you ride without pause!"

Talbot laughed in his face.

"You've come from Katherine, and your soul's sore.

9

Well, work it off on my host Featherhaugh then, I've no time."

He brushed past the giant, and mounted. Tim the hostler gazed up, frightened; Talbot tossed him a copper.

" 'Twould be well that ye rode past Abergavenny Lane without a pause," Gillard called.

Talbot turned in saddle. "Do you threaten me then, Tom Gillard? Wouldst ruffle, right here on the high-road? Nay, I'll get down and show you how a rapier should be used, if that's what ye seek."

"I've said my say."

"Oho! Then I'll say mine! Yes, I ride to London. But I stop to visit Katherine Abergavenny. And while I'm there I'll give her a ring to signify our troth. I'll give her more than that, Gillard. I'll tumble her right there in her own screens, to seal the bargain, eh? Think of that when you drink your wine, Gillard. It may help the taste."

He rode off.

CHAPTER TWO

As he rode up Abergavenny Lane, Talbot told himself that he'd been a fool. He should have played the diplomat. He should have smiled and been evasive; and this not for his own protection, nor yet that of Katherine—she was safe enough—but because of Katherine's father, that genial widower and fond parent, aged, somewhat deaf, increasingly weak, always interested in local sports and the breeding of his livestock. Yes, it was for William Abergavenny that he should have had consideration. This and only this was the reason why he and Katherine had not announced, months earlier, their determination to marry.

Everybody suspected it. Now Gillard knew. And Gillard was no bagpipes, all wind and noise. Whatever his bluster, he was by no means an empty threat. There were many ways in which he could hurt William Abergavenny.

Talbot should have controlled his temper. He should have held his tongue. He was becoming altogether too high-spirited and cocksure, now that he was a gentleman of the great world.

Kate's father, in the screens, startled him with congratulations.

"Katy's told me, Talbot, and there's not a man more pleased in this kingdom. For mark you, there was a time when I feared it might be that scowling hulk Gillard, who's been about here so much. He was here last night. Aye, and again this very afternoon."

He beamed near-sightedly.

"And d'ye know what Katy told him? Told him to be gone and not return. Told him she was sick of his glowering face, and that she wouldn't have him if he was the last man on earth, and that she was going to be your bride. Eh-eh! I overheard it. 'Twas how I learned. Katy says she'd've told me anyway."

"I had planned to ask you, sir, but—"

"Eh-eh! Don't be over-polite. For you know as well as I do that Katy would have her way even though I was to bellow objections for a week on a week. But I'd never object. Not when it's you she picked. You'll tarry the night, Talbot?"

"Nay. I can stay only a few hours. Milord of Sussex bade me speed, for he needs every blade he has, what with Leicester's men snarling and snapping at him."

"You mislike Leicester, eh? Well, that's a small matter to us out here. But if you've only got a few hours you'll not be wanting me to chatter the time away. There's a sick pig back in the stables I'll be having a peek at before it's too dark."

Then Katherine appeared.

She was tall and somewhat boyishly slender. Her hair was so very dark a brown that in some lights it could be taken for black; and her eyes were a dark hazel; while her mouth was red, small, serious. But then, her whole expression was one of seriousness. Just now, for all the simple taffeta, and for all the simplicity of her walk too, she looked so lovely, so stately and even queenly as she came down the dim old staircase, that Talbot knew with

12

a thrill that here was a woman who would grace any court.

Not that Katherine, as his wife, was likely to be called to the great court itself. Talbot knew this, and probably she knew it too. For Elizabeth was not fond of beautiful women who happened also to be the wives of handsome courtiers. Indeed, Talbot was tolerably certain—though he never mentioned this to Katherine—that their marriage would mark the end of his ambition to become a gentleman-pensioner in attendance upon the Queen herself. Such an appointment, now would mean that he would have to keep his wife far away, pretending to have lost interest in her because of his bedazzlement by the Queen's majesty. And this he had no intention of doing. For while he was a lively admirer of Elizabeth Tudor, and as patriotic as the next man, he could not at any time pretend that a bald, skinny, black-toothed, pockmarked female, for all the royal blood that might run in her veins, was a more desirable person than Katherine Abergavenny.

Katy went into his arms without hesitation.

"I told Father everything."

"Aye. He told me. He has gone out to nurse a sick pig."

"I told Tom Gillard too, this very afternoon."

"I too told Gillard myself, in front of the inn. Rest thy conscience, sweet. He was sure to know, and sure to be angry, no matter from whom he learned it."

"Father doesn't fear him. But I do—for Father."

He smiled, and kissed her again, palming her breasts. She permitted this, though she did tremble.

From his purse he fished forth a plain gold ring. It held a single sapphire, a very large one. It had cost eighteen crowns, only two of them being Talbot's own, the rest borrowed. He held it up.

13

This was not in the great-hall nor yet in the screens, or entrance-hall, of Abergavenny Manor. It was in the solar, a small, comfortably furnished family chamber, one no servant would enter unless on summons. No servant came now, for example, to light the candles, though it was dim in the solar, the sun having set.

"To match thine eyes," Talbot whispered, and slipped the ring onto her finger.

He was a forthright person, for all his courtly training. He did not beat about the bush.

"There's—there's *my* token. And now, what wilt thou give me in return?"

Another woman might have pretended puzzlement. Kate was too straightforward. She did try to get out of his arms, but she did not try very hard.

"No, dear," she whispered. "It would be a sin, until we're married."

"Why, so it would," he said. "All the same—"

He released her, and she did not move away from him. He strode to the door of the screens, the only one there was. He closed this door. He threw the bolt, so that it thudded into place.

"No, Talbot," she whispered. "No, we mustn't . . ."

He turned, facing her. He could scarcely see her as she stood there, her face white. He did not move, except to hold out his arms.

After a while she gave a sob, or it could have been a small glad laugh. She turned her back. With swift hands she began to undress.

Lolling among the cushions, lazy, naked, not touching one another, not even seeing one another in the darkness, they forced a return to practicality.

"John Gilbert's brother has returned from Ireland," Talbot told her. "He's been knighted, and he's near the

14

Queen. He loved my father. I'll speak to him."

"Dost think he can—"

"Monckton! Francis Monckton's the man! He could ask for anything but her crown, and she'd thrust it into his hands. He'd oust Leicester if he could. He's working for that. But he lacks a party."

"But surely, Talbot, thou'dst not—"

"Nay, sweeting. I'll not offer my own services to Frank Monckton. I'm Sussex's man, and that I'll remain. But Humphrey Gilbert is of no party. He teeters. And Monkcton's looking for just such men. So methinks a proper chat with Sir Humphrey, who for the love that he bore my father will make the request of Frank Monck-ton—methinks that this will leash the Gillard hound, eh? Monckton's his cousin, y'know. They told me at the inn that Monckton sleeps at Gillard's Elm this very night. And he's too great a power for even Tom Gillard to defy. Oh, thy father'll be safe enough, chuck! It only means a little work, a little whispering," he said.

In fact, it would mean much more. It would mean, for example, a considerable sum of money in bribes; and Talbot did not know where he could get money. But he told Kate nothing of this.

"Tom Gillard growls because he hopes it will frighten us. But when it's all over, sweet, he'll subside. I'll be back within the week. I swear it. Milord of Sussex has been expecting such a petition, and he'll grant it."

"Within the week," she whispered, and snuggled closer.

"And we'll publish the banns right here in Chagford. And after the joining, sweet, there'll be no man in all the world who'll be as happy as Talbot Slanning."

From where they lay they could see through a window the moon rising over Abergavenny Lane.

Kate stirred, and glanced toward the screens.

"Father takes a long time tending that pig."

"I make no doubt he's inspecting the stables again. He knows I have but a little time to spend with thee, and he is kind. Now, darling—"

"Should we, again?"

The moon had apologetically retreated behind a cloud when at last these two dressed and made their farewell. The mouldy old mansion was quiet.

William Abergavenny was not in the stables or in the stable yard when Talbot went out to saddle his horse. Talbot stopped at the front entrance for one final kiss.

"Father hath not returned," she whispered anxiously.

"He's tiptoed in by the kitchens and gone up to his own room. But if there's no light in his window I'll hallo him as I go down to the highroad."

Abergavenny Lane was a narrow and deep cut, lined with hedgethorns and tiny ferns and wild flowers. This night it was wet and slippery, the spicey odor of pinks sharp in the air, for there had been heavy rains in the afternoon; and because of this, and also because of the absence of moonlight, Talbot walked his mare toward the highroad. The lane, he knew from experience, was blotched with holes deep enough to trip any horse.

At the first sharp curve, from where he knew he could see the windows of William Abergavenney's bedchamber, he turned.

It was this turn that saved his life. For it faced him fairly into one of the men who sprang upon him from the bank.

CHAPTER THREE

Since there was somebody before him, he jumped back. He felt a jolt at his right elbow. Then something struck him from behind. The blow landed on his left shoulder.

They were coming both ways, eh?

He dropped to hands and knees, and another bludgeon caught him above the right ear and set his head singing. He rolled sideways, thumping against a pair of legs.

The space was narrow, the darkness complete. There was no room to draw, but Talbot did succeed in snicking out his dagger, and with this he slashed wildly at the legs. There was a screech of pain. Talbot rolled back— barely in time to miss another clubbing from above.

He got to his feet, cursing. Three blurred figures he saw, one of them very close. But now there was room to draw, and with a Spanish rapier in his fist Talbot Slanning would have laughed at twenty.

Even in that dark place the ruffians must have seen steel flash. Perhaps they had heard of the Slanning swordsmanship. Perhaps fighting any man face to face, whatever the odds, was not to their fancy. They disappeared into the foliage.

They went west, away from the highway. Talbot could

hear them crashing through the hedgethorn and scrambling up the steep embankment. He went after them.

"Stand, ye mongrels!"

Scratched and panting, he emerged upon the edge of an unexpectedly serene meadow, and paused. Three shadows, one of them limping behind the other two, were making for a little wood to the west. The highroad, and beyond it Deathick Wood, offered a nearer and safer shelter; but these fellows were hurrying back to their master, to the man who had sent them out. On the other side of that nameless clump of trees was Gillard's Elm.

All thought of being a diplomat, of being patient and evasive, was forgotten. Talbot, mad with rage, would have dashed across the meadow and straight for Tom Gillard's house, had he not at this moment heard a groan from the bushes behind him.

Back through the hedgethorn he crashed. He found William Abergavenny by the side of the lane not more than a few feet from the scene of the fight. The squire lay on his back. His head was sticky with blood, and he had been badly bruised and shocked, but a quick examination convinced Talbot that no bones were broken.

"I didn't see 'em . . . came at me from behind . . ."

"There's no need to see them, sir." Talbot's eyes were like frosted steel, and his mouth was taut. "I know where they came from."

The two staggered back to the manor house, the older man leaning upon Talbot, who shouted for Katherine to open the door. And soon there were servants everywhere, and William Abergavenny's wounds were being cleansed and bandaged.

"Was it Gillard? I'll send that—"

"Send nothing, sir," Talbot cried. "For within the hour he'll not be alive to receive it."

Katherine's father would recover: this was all Talbot wished to know, and he started away. Katherine came hurrying after him.

"Remember to be calm, and patient, and—"

"Piss on patience! There's been too much of it already!"

He pushed past her, and went with long strides down the soggy lane to the place where he had left his horse. Katherine ran after him, calling, "Talbot! Talbot, my love! *They'll kill thee!*"

But he had mounted, and was lost among the shadows.

Four minutes later Talbot was kicking the door of Gillard's Elm. A menial without livery opened for him, demanded his mission, and when Talbot would have pushed past him grabbed his shoulder. Talbot, outraged, punched the man squarely in the mouth. Talbot strode toward the light.

Thomas Gillard and his guest were sharing a decanter of wine in the great-hall, but were nevertheless seated close together and conversing in whispers. Their heads jerked around when Talbot stamped in, and both men rose. Gillard was truculent, accusing. But on the countenance of Sir Francis Monckton there was only polite astonishment and no alarm.

"Draw, you pirate! Have out here and now!"

Talbot's rapier appeared, exquisitely bright. Gillard, who seemed almost to have expected this, was not two seconds slower. He started toward Talbot as Talbot started toward him.

"Gentlemen, *stop!*"

The Queen's favorite stepped between them, a courageous act. Both his arms were raised. He had a manner. He was born to command. He had scarcely lifted his voice, yet the two points dropped, the swordsmen paused. Behind Talbot the punched servant, mouth bloody, eyes aflame, appeared with a halberd snatched from a panoply in the entrance hall, but him Monckton halted with a glance.

"Tut, gentles! Would ye brawl like drunken apprentices?"

He stood tall and keen, utterly cool. His voice was not mild, yet neither was it raspy. His head was stiff on a slender neck, and his eyes moved back and forth from one man to the other, while mentally he weighed the situation. He was an extraordinarily handsome man, and he knew it, as the Queen knew it, and indeed all England. But he must have sensed that the beauty of Leander and the prestige of Majesty itself would not prevent these two men from battling.

"At the least," Monckton said, "permit me, as an impartial witness, to hear the tale back of these high words." He addressed himself to Talbot, "You, sir? You fancy yourself wronged?"

Outwardly more quiet, Talbot told his story in spurts, hot and jerkily, concealing nothing. Francis Monckton listened in just-sympathetic-enough silence, nodding thoughtfully from time to time, his almond-shaped eyes fixed upon the speaker.

Afterward Monckton faced his host.

"You deny this, Tom?"

Gillard snarled, "I deny nothing and affirm nothing! He wishes to fight? Excellent! Let it be now! And here!"

"Tush, Tom. You're the drunken apprentice again."

The favorite stroked with a forefinger the crisp blond hairs at his chin. Presently he turned to bow before Talbot.

"It appears that you two will fight, whatever the provocation, eh?"

"Yes."

"Well, then, Master—uh—Master Slanning, if upon

20

your return to your lodgings you will dispatch a servant to—"

"I have no servant. I have no lodgings hereabout. And I seek no Morris dance, sirrah! I'll fight here and I'll fight now!"

"Good," Gillard said quickly.

Monckton was troubled. He was in Devonshire on a series of visits arranged for the purpose of forming a personal party in the coming Parliament, and he was attended only by four bodyservants, none of them gentle. In consequence, there was nobody to whom he could appeal. The prospect of a duel did not please him. The Queen had scant respect for the custom—"a waste of good swordsmen!"—and trouble of some sort surely would come out of this night's affray. The favorite himself, howsoever innocent, would be involved. The best he could do, he decided, was make the affair as nearly regular as was possible in the circumstances.

"Are ye village broilsters? There can be no such meeting in the house of one of the parties."

"We'll go outside," Gillard suggested.

Talbot nodded.

"But there's no spot that the rain hasn't reached!" Sir Francis Monckton cried.

"There's the Three Crowns," Gillard said. "Old Featherhaugh will not love it, I wot, but his long-room upstairs has a half-dozen of candle-branches, and the floor's firm and straight. You'll act for me, Frank?"

Francis Monckton smiled wryly, but with a resigned inclination of his head. He did not like to do this; but Thomas Gillard had county connections he could not afford to antagonize.

Yet he could insist upon the proprieties, and hope. He addressed Talbot.

"And you, sir?"

"Nay, I need no one."

"I'll not consent to act unless you are represented in the field, and by somebody of gentle blood!" Sir Francis said sharply.

Frowning, Talbot considered. He was impatient of all this fuss.

"There is my friend Robert Butterwalk. His station is sufficient."

"Ah, but do you suppose that this good Master Butterwalk will be at home tonight? And does he live hereabout?"

"He'll be at the Three Crowns," Talbot promised. "He always is, at this hour."

It dashed the favorite's final hope. Again he shrugged. He signaled to a menial.

"Call none of my own men, but you yourself fetch me my cloak and a mask."

For the sight of a man like Sir Francis Monckton in a public place like the Three Crowns might create such excitement as to make it hard to obtain privacy. Monckton did not wish to be recognized. There was yet a chance that this affair might end without killing; and if so, it could be kept quiet forever.

The favorite was garbed in what for him was humble attire. He wore a white brocaded doublet with a raised pattern, lined with pinkish lilac sarcenet. Down the front, from ruff to peascod, ran a row of pearl-cluster rosettes, eighteen of them in all. His black silk trunk-hose, like his black velvet sword-belt, was embroidered with gold lace. His rapier was an original Di Brescia, gold and polychromatic enamels, studded with diamonds, priceless, a prince's. Over all this he threw his Spanish cloak, pulling its broad sable collar close about his face. He tugged on a pair of buff leather gauntlets. He raised a mask.

22

"Come. Sheath first, for I'll have no brawling on the path. This side of me, Tom. And you, Master Slanning, take the other side." There was a wistful sigh in his voice.

CHAPTER FOUR

Robert Butterwalk grinned across an apple dumpling and a mug of cider. The cider was of the sort known locally as "rough," and was exceedingly strong—stronger than wine, as strong as French brandy.

"Is this what you call riding to London? Did I not predict—"

Then he saw Gillard and the masked stranger.

"Oh," he whispered. "You—you've been ruffling it, Tally?"

Talbot leaned close. There were fifteen or sixteen men in the room, and he did not wish to be overheard.

"Upstairs and now, Robin. Wilt act for me, eh?"

"I like it not. Can't we so arrange it that—" Robert Butterwalk rose, shaking his head.

"Nay, Robin. Fight I must, and now. Thou'rt sober?"

"Oh, aye. As any curate at a Shrove Tuesday Psalmsing. Upstairs, eh?"

He did not tell the strict truth. The shock of Talbot's announcement had made him seem sober and even feel sober; and in the general excitement nobody noticed that his step was not even, nor was his hand steady, as he mounted the stair.

The public room buzzed behind them. Old Feather-haugh fussed here and there, lighting candles from a taper that trembled as he held it. He had ordered his assistants away from the upstairs chamber, and garru-lously saw in person to the comfort of these unexpected guests. What it was all about he did not know, but he could make a tolerably accurate guess. Like everybody else in and around Chagford he had heard of the sharp words that afternoon between Talbot Slanning and Tom Gillard; and he knew both young men, had known them for years. A reconciliation, he was aware, was not a thing to be expected. It was more likely that this gath-ering meant violence—ordered, regulated murder.

"I will remain to attend your wants, gentlemen," he quavered.

The man behind the mask said with impeccable polite-ness: "Nay, good mine host, it will not be necessary."

There were six candle-branches with seven candles to the branch—wax candles too, not tallow. Featherhaugh lighted every one, dawdling over the job.

"One of my waiters, then? He could fetch some capon and dumplings, good milords? And wines—what wine would ye have, eh?"

"None," said the man with the mask.

"No wine."

"None. Pray leave us in peace, mine good host."

Featherhaugh flared, briefly, somewhat hysterically, forgetful of his training.

"Aye, *leave* you in peace, that I'll do! But is't your purpose to *remain* in that blessed state? I'll have no—"

"*Get out!*" Tom Gillard started toward him.

Featherhaugh got out. All of his employees and most of his customers of the night were gathered just out-side of the door, and he scattered them like geese, shushing them angrily, sending them back downstairs.

25

But he himself—*he* remained at the door! He heard
the bolt thrown from the inside, and heard somebody
shut the window curtains. He leaned against the door as
much for physical support as because he desired to get
his ear closer to the sounds; and his face was hot and
shiny with sweat, while his lips moved in prayer.

Sir Francis Monckton, when the bolt had been thrown,
lowered his mask and threw off his cloak.

"It is an honor to act with you, sir. I am Francis
Monckton, gentleman-pensioner to Her Gracious Majesty the Queen."

Robert was astounded. He blinked, mouth open, eyes
like saucers. But he managed to execute a bow.

"I am Robert Butterwalk, an esquire of Chagford,
sir."

Formally—Monckton with swift white fingers, Robert
with sweaty hands that shook—they examined each principal's doublet in order to be certain that neither wore a
brigandine or chain-mail undershirt. They compared the
swords. These were of the same length, each swept-
hilted, with long quillons, though Gillard's was slightly
heavier.

"It is your privilege, sir," Monckton told Talbot in a
voice that betrayed some hope, "to refuse to fight unless
these weapons be of exactly similar weight."

"I care not," Talbot said.

Nor did he. This was no gesture of bravado. Rapier-
fighting still was new in England, where many an old
warrior sneered at it as an effeminate importation.
Masters of the fence were not numerous, even in London. At the academy of one of these, Rowland Kirke,
Gillard had been a student, and had come to be rated as
a provost: this much Talbot knew. But Talbot himself
had studied under the greatest masters of all, the *spada-
cinos* of Italy, and notably under Viggiani and the in-

comparable Giovanni dell' Agocchie. To Talbot, therefore, the average Englishman with a sword was a blundering, stamping boy. So far from thinking that a heavy blade gave any advantage, Talbot believed in the lightest weapon commensurate with length and sturdiness.

Each man carried also a dagger with a thirteen-inch blade, which he was to be permitted to hold sword-fashion in his left hand, and to use, if he could, for parrying, or possibly, if the swords themselves were locked, for a death blow.

"It may not be amiss if you both see that my pistol's here also," Robert Butterwalk said, and produced the thing.

"Nay, put it away! Thou'lt be having it explode!" Talbot objected angrily.

But Francis Monckton, who had quite naturally taken over supervision of the affair, and who was the final court for all decisions, unexpectedly supported Robert. Indeed Monckton brought forth a tiny silver pistol of his own, and thoughtfully loaded it.

"Nay, Master Butterwalk is right. The representatives should be otherwise armed than with their blades. 'Tis the way they are doing it now in France."

Talbot, for his part, cared not a damn how they were doing it in France; he didn't like firearms. However, he was too eager to meet Gillard to keep up a complaint.

"You will stand at this end of the room, Tom. And you, Master Slanning, at this other end. So! You will both advance and engage when I call the signal. Then you will fight until one of you is unable to fight longer. Are you ready, gentlemen?"

Robert Butterwalk dumped fine powder into the priming pan of his pistol, and cocked the thing, and held it

27

horizontally, aiming at nothing. He blinked from one principal to the other.

"Are you ready, gentlemen?" he repeated after Monckton.

The long-room at the Three Crowns, Chagford, Devonshire, really was long—full forty feet, the same length as the inn itself. It was rectangular and perhaps eighteen feet wide. The floor was quartered oak, rich and smooth, but not slippery. The walls were paneled in oak, and the plaster ceiling was richly painted; but there was nothing that would reflect light in a disconcerting manner, nothing that would hamper the duel. Rich red curtains of Utrecht velvet covered the windows, which were set in a succession of canted bays over the street. At one end, Gillard's end, was an ornate fireplace, but there was no fire, for the May night was mild and warm. The candle-branches were set on small tables, regularly spaced, and the candles cast a full, even, quiverless light.

"Gentlemen?"

Talbot nodded impatiently.

Tom Gillard grunted.

"Draw, then! Advance and engage! And God be with you!"

Old Featherhaugh, as soon as he heard the first scrape of steel, started to pound the door. "*Stop, milords! Stop!*" Nobody paid any attention.

The master of Gillard's Elm came in quickly, with legs spread wide, like a man who wades through water. He held his rapier high, the point directed at Talbot's face. The dagger he kept close to his left hip, point out.

Talbot moved slower, heel-and-toing it with tiny steps. He held his guard low, the point raised. He was thinking that Gillard apparently was one of the older rough-and-tumble fighters, given to many passes, close engagement, much cutting and much beating of the blade. Such men might *look* ferocious, but they were easily handled by one who knew his weapon. Gillard at least would count upon his size and strength and greater reach.

Gillard tried four slashes for the head, which Talbot avoided easily by stepping back, though Talbot did not otherwise stir. This placed him near his end of the room, so that he did not dare to retreat much farther. And then, as he had expected, Tom Gillard, looking for a quick finish, thrust full-length.

Talbot parried without difficulty but found he could not free his blade for a riposte. Gillard had circled his point twice, pinning Talbot's guard to his own, so that their right hands, like their faces, were not more than an inch apart. But Gillard was not so fast with the dagger, and Talbot readily avoided that thrust.

Startled, scarcely believing that his attack had failed, Gillard released his pressure on Talbot's sword, and sprang back, raising his guard again.

Talbot smiled a slow, grim smile. He'd been at Tom Gillard's mercy for an instant there—had Gillard but known it!

But now, before Gillard could recover from his momentary confusion, Talbot Slanning moved in.

Death had come so close that he felt cold all over, as though the black angel actually had touched him in passing. This fellow was faster, cleverer, than Talbot had anticipated; and the fight must be carried to him.

"*Milords, open up, I pray you!*"

Robert Butterwalk waved his huge pistol and danced up and down in an agony of suspense and fright. His mouth was open, and he made curious little gurgling sounds in his throat.

The handsomest man in England remained motionless

29

and calm—all except his eyes, which danced with excitement.

Gillard, a bit bewildered by the brilliance of Talbot's counter-attack, retreated, parried, retreated farther, never getting a chance to riposte. It was a new experience for him to be backing away. Slowly, and with an even greater surge of anger than he had yet shown, he realized what he was doing. He grunted, and his chin sank a trifle. He stood against a rush, tried to parry with his dagger alone, and slashed at Talbot's head. The rapier caught only Talbot's dagger, causing sparks to fly, while Talbot's own blade licked in and out of the big man's left shoulder. Gillard fell back barely in time to save his life. Talbot's point, meant for the throat, grazed the Gillard chin instead, and blood began to pour from the cut, staining Gillard's beard.

Gillard's measure was longer than Talbot's—his arms and legs were longer. As he stood at bay, desperate, aware that the fireplace was close behind him, and that further retreat might be fatal, he was a dangerous man to try to reach. A trick was needed.

Talbot stooped far down, his swordguard low, his dagger high, and pretended to lose his balance, so that he was forced to put his right hand to the floor. His point was lowered, as though from the effort to recover balance.

Then Tom Gillard did exactly what Talbot had expected. He stepped on the swordblade with his left foot, pressing it against the floor, and at the same time swung high his right shoulder, raising his own sword for a terrific down blow.

Talbot was perfectly prepared for this. Gillard wore soft white leather slippers, and the floor was smooth oak. Talbot had figured that a jerk would free the blade and throw him far enough back to permit him to outstep

Gillard's blow and at the same time raise his point so that Gillard, by force of his attack, would be skewered upon it. A perfect example, Talbot thought, of the superiority of point over edge, rapier over broadsword.

Yes, he had estimated that a jerk would free the blade; but he had not supposed that it would free it without resistance; and he jerked mightily, with all his strength.

He never knew whether Tom Gillard had been off balance at that instant, so that his weight no longer was on his left foot, or whether Gillard with unaccustomed wit had seen through the trick and released that pressure purposely.

Whatever the reason, the blade came free with a tug; and Talbot, amazed, staggered half the length of the chamber, waving both arms wildly in an attempt to regain his balance.

Gillard, had he been prepared, could have ended the fight then and there. As it was, he paused a fleet second after his own blow had found only air. And when he did spring forward, cutting furiously, it was too late.

Talbot sat upon the floor with a bang. But he scrambled to one knee; and is sword arm was raised, his guard high, when Gillard's attack came. In that position he was safe enough. He could meet and parry any attack, though he could not return it until he had regained his feet.

But Robert Butterwalk could not comprehend this. To Robert, crazed by anxiety and excitement, befuddled still by the cider, it seemed that his friend was helpless, that Tom Gillard was about to slaughter a man who was down.

"Hi! You can't do that!"

He stepped forward, waving the pistol. Sir Francis Monckton sprang to his side, spun him around, threw up the pistol-arm.

"You fool! Put that—"

Nobody ever was to learn how it happened. The thing had been cocked and was hair-triggered, so perhaps the mere motion of Robert's arm was responsible.

Whatever the cause, the striker fell. There was a wheezy, whirring sound; a column of minute blue sparks rose briskly, slantingly, and the pan powder flashed. With a terrific roar the overcharged weapon was thrown up, so that the end of its barrel struck Robert on the chin, stunning him. And Sir Francis Monckton went over backward—went rapidly, full-length, as though shoved by a mighty hand. The little silver pistol he had held tinkled on the floor like some forgotten bit of jewelry. The ruff and the upper part of the beautiful white doublet were blackened by gunpowder. The face, too, was utterly black, except for the wide-staring eyes. The throat was torn, though it seemed unable to bleed, perhaps because the blast had cauterized it.

Robert Butterwalk was motionless, too dazed to understand what had happened.

Tom Gillard instinctively stepped back several paces before he lowered his point.

It was Talbot who went to the body. He leaned close to the hideously twisted and blackened face, and stared into those sightless eyes. He thrust a hand under the doublet. He looked up.

"Dead."

Yellow-gray smoke moved languidly about and stretched itself with a feline display of indifference. Echoes of the explosion batted to rest in remote corners. The hammering on the door and the shouts of the men outside in the street had ceased. The world was all one silence.

"The Queen worshipped that man," Tom Gillard said in a flat expressionless voice.

He grabbed a chair, and with it smashed the glass out of one of the windows. He put a hand on the sill, and vaulted, disappearing below. Somebody in the street screamed. A horse galloped away.

"He's right," Talbot yelled. He took Robert in both arms and dragged him to the shattered window. "There's one chance!"

They landed asprawl. Somebody was silhouetted in the open inn door, waving his arms, shouting something. Tim the hostler was on the ground, his hand pressed against his right cheekbone, while blood oozed between his fingers.

Robert's horse was back in the stables, unharnessed, and there would be no time to get it. But Talbot and Gillard and the late Sir Francis Monckton had been careful to leave their steeds saddled and loosely tethered at the hitching-post. Gillard's was gone, but Talbot's Spanish jennet still was there, and so was Monckton's black Hungarian.

"Haste, Robin!"

The plump youth moved as though in a stupor. He had said never a word. For a full five minutes, while they slushed through mud, he stared blankly before him, not even touching the reins.

"We—Where are we going?" he gasped at last.

"France."

"I'll ride to Exeter. I'll get the sheriff. I'll tell him everything. Thou hast no need to—"

"Go to! There'd be no questions and no trial! It comes to high treason, and whoever was in that room tonight would be strapped to the rack—with a halter for what survived. Ride, man!"

Yet at the entrance to Abergavenny Lane Talbot himself came to a halt.

"I'll turn here. Rack or no rack, I'll not quit England without a word to Katherine. Ride on, Robin."

"Nay, I'll wait for thee."

Abergavenny Manor was dark, silent. Starlight drizzled half-heartedly upon its roofs and gables, and there was an air of drowsy comfort about the whole place. Many times afterward, in strange remote places, Talbot was to remember the manor as it looked that night—placid, pallid, homelike, peaceful.

He left his horse at a turn of the lane and ran to the south side of the house. Both of Katherine's windows were open. He rattled the trellis which rose to one of them, and soon she appeared.

"Come down! The side door—hurry!"

She asked no questions, and a moment later he had her in his arms.

"There's been fighting? But thou'rt not hurt! Oh, Talbot!"

Tears rolled down her cheeks, and she stood very close to him, touching him here and there as though she wished to assure herself that he really was alive.

"The wrong man was hurt," he said somberly. "Aye, and killed. Frank Monckton."

At first she did not understand. She was not interested in Sir Francis Monckton, and her relief at finding Talbot safe and uninjured had left her dizzy, weak. He shook her gently. His voice was low, urgent.

"Didst hear, sweeting? Monckton was killed. *Killed!* Francis Monckton himself."

She stepped away, her eyes showing almost black in the darkness. She drew breath as though it was hot and hurt her.

"We go to France—Robin Butterwalk and I."

"I'll go with thee!"

"No. For the sake of thy father, if for no other reason,

34

thou must remain here. They father and thyself, chuck, should have no cause to fear."

Her eyes grew bigger. Her mouth fell open.

"No cause to fear?" Her voice was higher now, shriller. "No cause to fear? And thou, my love, sailing in a robber vessel to a foreign land, and leaving—"

He put a hand over her mouth, an arm around her shoulders, and he held her this way, very close, while she struggled. When she had subsided, sobbing, he released her gently, and kissed her.

Calmer, she patted her belly.

"Talbot, what if thou hast seeded me?"

"I'll send for thee, of course. And the babe. Just a little time, chuck. A little time to allow the Queen's rage to blow over."

There was no breeze, and the night was still. He He could hear something now, however. He could hear, from the direction of the village, the wet slap of hoofs, the squeal of saddle leather. They were coming after him.

"Good-bye, my darling. I'll always love thee."

He kissed her just once more, and then he ran.

CHAPTER FIVE

For three days Robert Butterwalk had scarcely spoken, scarcely moved, until Talbot began to fear that his companion's mind, admittedly never keen, was quitting him.

"Look up, look up, Robin, for the love of God! 'Tis bad enough, I wot, without glooming about it by the hour."

Robert managed a feeble nod.

"France . . ." he muttered.

Only a few times in his life had he been even so far away from his home as Plymouth, where they now lay, and he was not able to imagine a foreign land. The thought of travel, adventure, did not exhilarate him.

"France . . . I'm a murderer."

"Nay, thou'rt no murderer, man! An accident's not murder! Look up, Robin! 'Twill all be well soon enough. The Queen's Majesty will forget it, and in time we'll come slipping back."

Robert did not believe this, and in fact neither did Talbot himself. Elizabeth, by Grace of God Queen of England and Ireland and France, Defender of the Faith, etc., was no such short-memoried person as Talbot made pretense to think her. She was a Tudor, and a woman to boot; and she would seize the men who played any part in the death of Francis Monckton, no matter what the work and expense involved, no matter how long the wait. Talbot himself, in his heart, despaired of ever seeing England again.

For three days they had lingered in this bare, close, uncomfortable room above Ned Crocker's wineshop on the Barbican. Only twice in that time had they moved, on warning from Crocker, who conducted them to a nearby cellar while royal sergeants searched the wineshop building. It had been easy to guess that the fugitives would make for Plymouth; for in that resort of smugglers and pirates, Huguenots, beggars of the sea, and merely local desperadoes, lay their one chance of escape. So Plymouth was being scoured for them. The window of the room in which they sat had heavy curtains across it; nor did Robert and Talbot even after dark dare to light a candle.

"Eh, and I wonder if Tom Gillard's got away? He has friends in this port, and his own shallop."

Robert made no answer, and did not seem to have heard. Talbot shook him.

"Look up, lad! You can't quit before they've caught us! Suppose I venture out along the water front and hook you a doxie? A sixpenny bit ought to do it, if you don't mind one that stinks."

"What would I do with a wench?"

"God's feet! What anybody else would, of course. I wouldn't stay here and watch. I'd go downstairs and talk with Crocker."

"No."

"I just thought it might make you feel better."

"No."

There was a knock at the door. Talbot stiffened. Even Robert Butterwalk rose and quietly drew his sword. Talbot signaled for him to post himself on the far side of the door. Rapier and dagger drawn, Talbot called in a low voice:

"Who's there?"

The answer was faint, muffled. Talbot crossed to the window, opened it wide, and pushed back the curtain. He glanced at Robert, who nodded. Then he went again to the door. He unlatched the door and threw it open, stepping back as he did so.

An ape of a man entered. A curiously pale fellow, almost as broad as he was long, he wore a black leather jerkin, huge brown pantaloons, a brown felt hat. Much of his face was hidden by a yellow beard, the hairs of which went in every direction. His eyes were tiny, blue, shrewd. Enormous brass rings dangled from his ears.

"Ah, Captain Vaarts!"

They sheathed their weapons. Talbot closed the door.

Vaarts was a Dutchman produced by the all-knowing and well-paid keeper of the wineshop downstairs, Ned Crocker. He owned a small and very fast galleass, and he knew the Narrow Seas as well as they themselves knew the drift-lanes of Devon. He was willing, for a consideration already agreed upon and paid, to take them to France.

"Careful men, eh? Careful fellows."

Vaarts's eyes, so tiny as to be almost lost in the shadow between hat brim and whiskers, moved back and forth. He nodded. Possibly he grinned: it was difficult to be sure of this.

Talbot shrugged. He went to the window and closed it. "We did not know who it was. Is the boat ready?"

"*Ja.* Und ter tide goes oudt in half an hour. *Ja.*"

"Good!" Talbot and Robert made for their cloaks. "We'll start now, eh?"

"*Nein.* First, I must haff more money."

Talbot scowled. Already they had given this skipper

38

every coin Ned Crocker had left them (Talbot's offer to hire a whore for his friend had been more playful than practical, since it was not likely that they had a whole sixpence between them. They'd never seen Captain Vaarts before, and they knew they were endangering their lives when they made a contract with him for transportation to the continent. He might yet take them just outside of Plymouth Sound and there murder them, weight their bodies, and toss them overside, rather than risk conveying men who were obviously fugitives from the law. It had happened that way before.

"You've been paid," Talbot said coldly.

"*Ja*. I am an hones' man. I take you where I tell you I take you, *ja*. Put t'en I dit not know who you were."

"Oh, you know now, eh?"

"*Ja*. Und t'e price iss more."

He went to the window, cautiously withdrew the curtain, and pointed to a pair of thick-set, watchful men who loitered in the light of a cresset.

"Everywhere t'ey look for you. Such a mens I muss charge more. *Ja wohl*."

They could not be angry. They had previously accounted themselves fortunate that they were able to pay for passage and also pay Crocker the go-between. They'd had little enough. They could not blame Vaarts for demanding more, now that he knew they were not ordinary petty criminals but the very pair of men whom all England was searching for in the name of an angry Queen.

"But we have no more money."

Vaarts shrugged, and the rings in his ears waggled back and forth.

"T'en I not take you."

He tossed a leather purse upon the table.

39

"I am hones'. We make no trip. *Ju.*"

He turned to go.

"Wait!"

Talbot unstrapped his sword-belt, tossed sword and dagger and belt upon the table.

"It's from Madrid. I bought it there myself, at the workshop of Sebastian Hernandez. Does that mean anything to you, Captain Vaarts? There's not a finer brace of blades in all the world."

He might have overpraised the weapons, but it was true that they were beautiful, and valuable, and that he had purchased them from a celebrated armorer in the days when he still supposed himself to be rich.

The seaman's eyes glittered. He knew nothing of the art of these weapons—a stout broadsword or a cutlass would be more familiar to him, and he regarded these things on the table as the fancy toys of fancy gentlemen —but he did know true Toledo when he saw it. More, he knew gold. He knew the worth of seed pearls, a multitude of which were set along the quillons of these matched blades. And diamonds: there was a small diamond set into the hilt of each weapon.

He picked the things up, fondled them. They were exquisite articles, and went to the heart of this rude fellow.

"*Ja, Ja!* I take t'em. *Ja.*"

He started to strap the sword-belt about his own waist, but Talbot discreetly pointed out that he was not wearing a long cloak and that a sea captain with such weapons surely would attract attention.

"When we get to France you'll have them," said Talbot.

"*Nein!* When we get on t'e ship!"

"All right. Now lead the way."

There were preliminary instructions, for Vaarts was a careful worker. They were to follow him but not too closely. At no time, until they were safe under decks, were they to address to him a single word. And if on the way there was any sort of trouble—street brawls were not uncommon in seaports, he pointed out—they should not expect him even to recognize them, much less help them.

"Ja. We go t'em. On t'e ship you giff me t'em stickers. Ja."

He departed, and a few moments later Robert and Talbot strolled after him. Their cloaks were close about them, and they had turned the collars high. It was raining a little, and it was early evening. The way down to the docks was crowded with apprentices, prostitutes, merchants, mariners, jugglers, pedlars, clerks. The Catwater itself was crammed with shipping—galleys, crumsters, shallops, caravels, hoys, here a high-sided galleon loaded with pepper and cloves and indigo from the Portuguese Indies, there huge carrack or a buff-bowed phlegmatic merchantman from the Low Countries. There were smugglers' vessels and Flemish and Huguenot pirate craft and hundreds of small rowing pinnaces. Rigging was a mad maze against the evening sky.

Twice they passed royal sergeants who wound in and out of the crowds, hawk-eyed.

Vaarts turned suddenly to the right and made for a stone quay to which half a dozen small vessels had been moored. Robert and Talbot, starting after him, were stopped by a group of seamen, one of them, a monstrous bellowing fellow, very drunk indeed.

"Oho! Who be these fine scrimps?"

He pushed Robert Butterwalk, who staggered back against Talbot. Talbot bit his lip angrily; but his quick temper already had caused much woe, and now above all times, he told himself, he must keep it in control.

"Quietly, Robin . . . Walk around him," Talbot whispered.

41

The big fellow stood squarely in their path, swaying.

"Have over, Matt, and come to the ship with us," one of his companions pleaded, "for if we lose the tide the skipper'll have a cat across us."

Robert started to walk around the trouble-maker, giving him all the room possible. But his foot slipped in the mud, and in an effort to regain his balance he fell against the mariner.

"Oho! 'Tis a ruffle you'd have, eh?"

The mariner hit Robert with a huge red fist just over the left ear, and Robert fell to hands and knees.

Talbot forgot his good intentions. He punched the mariner twice in the face. Matt, grunting, more amazed than hurt, retreated several steps. He stared foolishly at Talbot, and blinked a moment. Then, as his head cleared, and he began to feel warm blood forming inside of his mouth, and to understand what had happened, he roared like some stabbed beast and charged with both fists flying.

Three times Talbot struck him, each time jolting the big head back. But this was a brute, unfeeling, mad. It charged again; and Talbot in desperation ducked, grabbed the man around the knees, and lifted suddenly with all his strength. The seaman was slammed back against a stone hawser-post; and after that the seaman did not stir.

Robert was shaking his head, trying to clear his brain, trying to rise. Talbot shuffled close to him but did not dare reach down to help him. For the mariners were on all sides. A few had bludgeons, and Talbot saw at least two sheath knives.

"Aside, clods," he said coldly. "My friend and I will go down to that quay, and whoso tries to stop us I'll kill him on the spot."

It might have impressed a crowd of West Smithfield

roughs, but it was the wrong way to talk to men of the sea.

"He hurt Matt Coppledick!"

"A high-and-mighty lord, eh? Tells us to get out of his way!"

"He hurt Matt! Are we going to stand here and see him hurt Matt?"

Talbot had neither time nor space in which to draw. A club struck his neck from behind. Another glanced off his right temple, drawing a gush of hot blood. And then its fairly rained blows. Talbot twisted, turned, punched. He found himself on his knees. He caught a flash of a knife, and squirmed aside barely in time to spare his shoulder its bite. Somebody kicked him in the face.

"Back, swine! 'Tis fifteen minutes to the turn of the tide, and I find ye fighting in the streets! Back!"

Everything became quiet. Talbot, his ears ringing, his mouth and nose running blood, lurched to his feet.

In the center of a circle of attentive seamen was a very short fellow with a deep loud disagreeable voice. He was scarcely thirty, but clearly he was accustomed to obedience. Speckless black leather boots encased his legs, and his feet were spread wide. He had a damn-you manner. His doublet was black and it glittered with pearls. His velvet trunk hose were dark purple, and so too was the gold-slashed Spanish cloak that hung from his left shoulder. He carried no weapon save a dagger, silver-hilted and encrusted with rubies. He was a thick man, a man it would not be easy to budge. On his round head was a smart Venetian morion, which glistered furiously in the light of torches. His face was red, his beard a reddish-yellow and very stiff. His eyes were a steely blue-gray.

"Matt Coppledick, eh? Badly hurt?"

Two of the men knelt beside the trouble-maker, examining him with their hands. "Shoulder's broken, sir," one said.

"Blessed be God, blessed be the Lord. Take him home, you two. And mind you're back within minutes or I'll have half the skin slashed off your backs."

He scowled at Talbot.

"You did this, eh? Matt Coppledick was one of the heartiest hands I had. Worth two ordinary men. And now, when all's set for us to sail, you must be a-breaking of his shoulder. Louts! Well, you'll do the work he was to have done—and you'll do it without pay! The two of you!"

Clearly he did not understand that he was addressing gentlemen. Talbot and Robert were wrapped from neck to ankle in cloaks bespattered with mud; their boots were masses of mud as well; and their broad-brimmed hats, crushed low on their heads, showed little of their faces.

"If you'll but listen—" Talbot started.

"No time!"

The Captain addressed the men at large, pointing to Robert and Talbot.

"Take them to the *Pascha*. I've authority, don't fear. Hasten, ye wine-sogged limbs!"

Something that seemed soft struck the back of Talbot's head as he tried to say something else. Dizzy, he spun around, raising his fists. It was a mistake. As from a great distance he heard the Captain's voice.

"And don't beat them so that they'll be of no service, ye blundering dogs!"

Then blackness came like a roaring, freezing wind.

CHAPTER SIX

The Captain was pleased with himself as he sat sipping canary and nibbling the last bit of bread he would know for many months. He stared through the stern windows at the twenty-five ton *Swan*. Beyond the *Swan*, cloudy gray in the early morning light, was the diminishing blur of Mount Edgcumbe.

The Captain was contented. Once more he was master of himself and of the men about him. At sea there were no commissioners, no politicians, no quibbling investors. The last few weeks had been especially trying, for orders had come, then counter-orders, then counter-counter-orders. It seemed for a time that all the world was in conspiracy to stop this voyage, possibly because all the world was suspicious of it.

Two persons only knew the Captain's plans—himself and a woman. The woman, being a woman, had blown hot and cold. In the morning, filled with enthusiasm, she had smiled upon him, but by afternoon fear had gripped her again and she was informing him by royal messenger that he must use his ships for the protection of Ireland. Ireland! He had nothing but contempt for that business, just as he had no respect for the petty robbers of the

45

Channel, who would cut any designated throat for a handful of copper. Ireland was not for him, nor the Sleeve either. Vultures might hover there. An eagle should fly far away.

Papers! Papers! He had been inundated with them. Seals, ribbons and signatures, sent by Secretary This or Clerk That, commanding one thing, countermanding it immediately afterward, blocking the prospect, unblocking it, the next day blocking it again. Until the previous night the Captain, for all his careful preparations, had not been sure whether he would be permitted to sail. Even at the very last minute there had been a threat of hitch. Some of the men had got drunk, and he himself had gone ashore and out into the streets to round them up in time to catch the tide. There had been a brawl— there always was!—and Matt Coppledick's shoulder was broken. With minutes counting like months, the Captain had done something he did not like to do and ordinarily would not have done. He had impressed the nearest two among the brawlers. No doubt they would prove to be lily-handed. They'd looked pale, wan. Well, they would learn. What's more, he would make them rich men —or corpses.

There was a shout, and scuffling on the deck, and the steel-gray eyes, which had been softly reminiscent, hardened. Right outside of his own cabin! Insolence!

The door flew open.

A slim blond young man with blue eyes and a pale face burst into the cabin. His clothes were splattered with mud and blood, and dried blood was clotted at his mouth. His face shone with sweat. His eyes were spurts of anger.

"Are you the captain of this boat?"

Francis Drake did not stir. He glanced at the three men who would have followed this young stranger into the cabin. He glanced just once—they froze on the threshold.

"I am the captain of this ship, yes. And the admiral of the fleet. And in future thou'lt remove thy hat when addressing me, and thou'lt call me 'sir.' "

The young man, curiously unimpressed, pounded the table.

"Don't 'thou' me," he stormed. "I know not what your filthy sea custom is, but I do know that it is no custom of mine to submit when ruffians lay hands on me and rob me of my sword."

"You carry a sword?" Drake sat up.

Cold and stern, inwardly he was troubled. For he saw now that this was no clerk but a person of gentle blood. Hot blood, too. And there was no greater snob in the world than Francis Drake.

"I *did* carry a sword, sirrah! And I demand that it be restored to me and that the men who assaulted me be punished and that my companion and myself be set down in France or else transferred to the first ship we meet that is sailing for the Continent."

"Why d'ye wish to go to France?"

"That's my concern, not yours. 'Tis enough for you to see that we get there without delay. After that I'll hear your apology."

Francis Drake leaned over the table and twisted his wine cup around and around. A horrid suspicion was forming in his mind. If there could be anything worse—

"You talk loftily. Who are you?"

For the first time the young man hesitated.

"I think I know. You are either Master Talbot Slanning, gentleman-pensioner to the Earl of Sussex, or else you are Master Robert Butterwalk of Chagford in Devonshire."

"Yes," Talbot said quietly.

47

He sat down, unbidden. He closed his eyes, and passed hands heavily across them.

"Yes, I am Talbot Slanning. And my companion is Robert Butterwalk. And we are both very dirty, thanks to your scoundrels."

"Oh," said Francis Drake.

He looked at the men in the doorway.

"Begone, Tom. Tell Master Oxenham to keep the course we've set. And see that every inch of canvas is spread, even to sewing on bonnets. We hail nothing and we respond to no hail, clear?"

"Aye, aye, sir."

Amazed, Talbot asked: "You're not taking us back?"

"No. And neither am I taking you to France or the Low Countries. I'll run no risk of this enterprise being blocked again."

"But, where do we go then?"

"We go to the Spanish Indies."

The Spanish Indies! America! The far fabulous land of screaming savages, hurricanes, poisonous jungles . . . the very other side of the world! Talbot sprang to his feet.

"But this is madness! I've no wish to go to the Indies!"

"That I much regret. You're going, nevertheless. Sit down, Master Slanning, and I'll tell you about it."

They restored Talbot's sword—Robert's also, though Robert was too seasick to care. They accepted them as gentlemen-adventurers, unexpected but by no means unwelcome members of the band. No mention ever was made of the death of Sir Francis Monckton. Very formally Captain Drake introduced Talbot to the others who sat above the salt at the *Pascha's* table: his own brother Joseph, Ellis Hixom, a grinning young shipbuilder's son from Dartmouth, and John Oxenham, a Devonshire squire. They drank toasts; they said grave things gravely;

they were very polite. However, none of them offered to tell Tablot to what part of the Americas they were going or what they meant to do when they got there, and soon he came to realize that in fact none of them *knew* this—none except the Captain himself, whom they trusted.

He was an odd, somber little fellow, that Captain. Though hardly sociable in ordinary circumstances, he did sit talking with Talbot after the others had left the table that first day at sea.

"We have prayers every morning and every evening on the forward deck," he announced. "You can recite prayers?"

"I—I have never tried."

"You will learn," the Captain promised.

He studied Talbot for some time, making Talbot uneasy.

"We'll have to find something for you to do during the long days, Master Slanning. Some work, some duty, eh?"

Talbot looked around, and waved a vague hand.

"I suppose I could help you to command the ship," he said.

The Captain almost smiled.

"I see that you are like so many other landsmen and think that the sailing of a ship's a task anybody could learn in an afternoon. But a lifetime's needed, Master Slanning."

Talbot shrugged. Like most of his friends, he had no high respect for ships and sailing-men.

"I am a courtier," he said, smiling a little. "I have been acting as confidential messenger for my Lord of Sussex, but here aboard the *Pascha* I take it that no messengers are needed?"

"Do you speak Spanish?"

49

"A few words. But I've forgotten most of it."

"You must know how to do *something!*"

Talbot didn't see why; he knew many men who did nothing at all and were very happy at it. He hesitated, looking around.

"Well, I was always esteemed an uncommonly good wrestler, and I have yet to meet the man who is my equal with a rapier."

"Ah!"

"I wrestle in the Devonshire manner, but I'm not opposed to the ruling-out of kicks. You yourself saw what I did to Coppledick, even when I was cumbered by a cloak."

"And the rapier?"

"I studied it in Spain and Italy. Viggiani of Bologna did me the honor to rate me a provost, and Giovanni dell' Agocchie, the great *spaducino* of Venice, twice said that I should take my place as a master indeed, did I but persist. I studied more briefly, too, under Camillo Agrippa, when I was in Rome, and under Giacomo di Grassi at Modena."

Francis Drake rose, rubbing his hands together.

"Now, this is good to hear! I have long wished to learn the Spanish method of sword-fighting. 'Tis said they are much superior to the English, for we rely too heavily on the edge. These Italians—are they comparable to the dons?"

"Far better. For, look ye," Talbot drew, "the gentlemen of Madrid favor greatly the *guardia bassa* and are prone to parry with the blades crossed as after a *passo obliquo,* which makes for too slow a riposte. But one who practices the Italian method will rather favor keeping his blade *di sopra,* unless—"

Francis Drake was a practical man.

"Nay, nay," he cried. "Fog me not with those foreign

words, but come out on deck and show me with the very weapons themselves, eh? I've some blunted blades here, and bracers and caps."

Mariners gathered in curiosity as Captain Drake ordered a space cleared in the waist, the only level stretch of deck. Talbot, while he affixed his bracer, noted again that all the hands were young. He did not see a man even among the officers who looked older than twenty-five, and many were in their teens. Captain Drake himself, he was to learn, though master of his own vessel for ten years, was not yet thirty.

"Art ready, Master Slanning? Now, if I was to attack this way . . ."

He seemed interested only in assault, never in defense. He came in clumsily. Talbot engaged the blade, turned it up, and touched the Captain at the heart. Puzzled, the Captain tried again. This time Talbot caught the blade high, deliberately waited for the second stroke, turned that stroke in such a manner that Captain Drake almost toppled, and again touched. He scarcely moved to do this.

"You must teach me that trick," the Captain muttered.

He was the perfect pupil. He tried hard, and was tireless and quite astoundingly strong. Best of all, he seemed never to feel ridiculous, even with the whole crew watching. Talbot knew that for all the awkwardness, here was a born fighter, a man who truly loved combat, and who, despite his unsmiling countenance, was thrilled when he faced another man with drawn steel. The hardest thing to teach him, Talbot was sure, would be the art of retreating.

It was Talbot who tired first.

"We must have many such lessons," the Captain said. "We will meet here every morning just after prayers, and again in the middle of every afternoon."

In this way the teaching of swordsmanship came to be Talbot's chief pastime aboard the *Pascha*, for not only the Captain but also Joseph Drake and John Oxenham and Ellis Hixom frequently engaged with him. But the Captain was the most persistent. His was of a hard-hitting nature and one to which the rapier would always be alien; but he stuck to it; when in doubt, he would simply put his head down and charge.

"You slash overmuch," Talbot told him repeatedly. "Use the point more, the edge less. When you draw back the blade for a cut you're out of guard position for an instant, isn't that so? And any good swordsman can pink you before that cut descends—aye, and be back out of your measure when it *does* descend."

"There might be much in what you say, Master Slanning. But in actual affray it would seem little satisfaction to stick steel into a man. It seems more natural to raise that steel and strike him with it."

"Natural? You should be controlled by your brain, Captain, not your muscles or your feelings. You must never make any move that emotion suggests. Otherwise you would respond to every feint and fall into every trap. Natural? Yes, perhaps the edge *is* more natural. But is the sword a natural weapon in the first place, sirrah? Do the beasts of the field have swords?"

The Captain wiped sweat from his face, while he examined the set of the main top; but he was giving much thought to Talbot's words.

"Hm-m . . . Yet in the Book, Master Slanning, it distinctly says that the Israelites under Joshua at Rephidim *smote* the Amalakites, not that they *struck* them."

"Maybe they didn't know any better then?"

Flippancy was foreign to Francis Drake, who resented it.

"Master Slanning, it is not the custom aboard of this vessel to question the word of God."

"Oh, I didn't mean that, sir! I only meant—"

"I'll check the quotation, but I'm sure it says 'smote.'"

And he retired to his cabin.

CHAPTER SEVEN

For all this, and with Robert sick most of the time despite good weather, Talbot found the days dragging. He moped. He walked aimlessly around the decks, getting in the way of mariners.

Because everything was so slow, and the sea so monotonous to the sight, he began to think about himself—for the first time in many years. He'd been busy lately, ever since he was a boy.

Well, here he was, going he knew not where nor for what purpose. Intended for a country gentleman, he had gone journeying on the Continent, where he picked up some education and a good many expensive habits; and there his ambition was to become a great soldier, a great captain of troops. When his father died and Talbot learned that his fortune was reduced to a handful of silver, he had to change those plans. Generalship cost money. Through influential friends he had obtained a post in the household of the Earl of Sussex, a man he immediately liked. There, in the court, his talents and tastes were convenient, expected. He found himself a swanking ruffler, a youth who wore pearls in his ears and bowed from the hips and argued about the merits of his

favorite perfume or his favorite mistress, a dandy ready
to fight even for a lie seven times removed.

Marriage to Katherine Abergavenny would have
changed all this, making him steadier, if less sensa-
tional, a prospect to which he had been reconciled. As
her husband, probably he would have become, in time, a
minor official of some sort, a fusser with state papers,
a country magistrate, an affixer of seals, with the odor
of tape and hot wax always about him.

Then the discharge of a pistol in the hand of a drunken
friend—and here he was in the middle of the Atlantic,
sword-instructor for a group of desperate adventurers
making for the unknown world of America, while back in
England half the law officers of the land were running
about in search of him, and Kate Abergavenny quite possibly was carrying his child.

It was a great change, and he was not sure that he
liked it. Hard riding he had known, and miserable inns,
and many a fight, but never had he expected to endure
the discipline of a ship at sea—the dull dry food, the
stink of bilge and squashed bugs, the lack of all the
creature comforts to which he had been accustomed.

What had he meant to be? He didn't know, really. Not
this, though—a fugitive! a misfit! a *teacher!*

From boredom and in an attempt to forget his own
worries, he began to take an interest in the way things
were done aboard the *Pascha.* He talked with the crew,
and sometimes even worked side by side with them. A
few still regarded him with black suspicion and dislike,
for Matt Coppledick had been popular; but most of them
were glad to chat. Indeed, Talbot's familiarity with the
hands, and his friendliness, somewhat shocked Captain
Drake.

For the Captain, though scrupulously fair, and comparatively gentle in the matter of punishments, was never

democratic. He feared to be. In all his dealings with the crew there was evident a consciousness of his position. Moreover, his cabin was sumptuously furnished, and his supply of clothes appeared to be without limit. Each morning he would strut in a different doublet, and he changed and experimented continuously with samite, sarcenet, taffeta, gold lace, silver lace, bombast, with boot hose and base hose and French short hose, and galligaskins and pantouffles, gamashes, and venetians.

It amused Talbot to observe that while the Captain avoided any reference to the killing of Sir Francis Monckton, preferring apparently to keep up the fiction that he did not know that his unexpected passengers were in any way connected with that event, still this peacock was not able to keep from asking Talbot—oh, so casually! —if he had ever met that personage. And when Talbot confessed, with equal carelessness, that it had once been his privilege to meet the late Sir Francis, the Captain plied him with eager questions about the appearance of the favorite, a celebrated clothes horse, and his dress and manner. Master Slanning had taken no particular note of Sir Francis's doublet? A pity! And the sleeves? Were they bishops or leg-o'-mutton? The Captain himself favored leg-o'-muttons, but he was anxious to know how the gentlemen of the court viewed this question, and specifically Master Slanning himself.

A strange little man. He never smiled. He was solemn at all times, though never pompous.

Talbot's new interest in matters nautical pleased and even flattered the Captain, conscious, as all his kind were, of the contempt of the rest of the world. Drake showed him how to handle an astrolabe and cross-staff, and how to check altitude findings with Johan Muller's tables of the sun's declination. Too, he lectured enthusiastically if not always intelligibly upon topsails, main courses, clew-garnets, leach-lines, forebowlines, falls, preventers, swifts.

"This is real," he would cry, stamping on the deck. "This is no mere pile of boards. Heed ye, Slanning! You tell me that the edge is passing and that soon men will fight only with the point?"

"Aye. And he who knows this before most of his fellow-men—he will have an advantage over those who depend on the broadsword strokes."

"Ah! And is not that the very thing I say about ships?" The gray eyes were shining, the face was very red indeed. "You are a swordsman, and I am a mariner, and I tell you that the ship itself should be the weapon—aye, and will be! Who has regard for a mariner except when there are goods to be transported? Who considers him in warfare? When a fleet is equipped and sent forth to battle, who commands? A soldier always, is it not? And which are given precedence aboard, the soldiers or the sailing-men?"

"The soldiers, of course."

"Aye. And when that fleet meets the enemy, upon whom is reliance placed? The soldier again! And why? Because these military men know nothing about ships and suppose that a battle at sea is to be conducted as nearly as possible like a battle on land. So they move this way and that, always with *land* tactics, expecting the seamen merely to obey orders like so many servants. They wish to get close and board. Hand-to-hand fighting —that's all they understand! But I tell you that with enough cannon and powder, and with gunners who know their business, and a real mariner commanding, a stand-off fight is better every time! Never get close! You keep telling me that when we fence."

"But the galleys! Think of Lepanto! Has not Giovanni Doria demonstrated once and for all that—"

"The Mediterranean! Don't talk to me of that puddle!" Drake swept his arms in a circle. "Pour a hundred Mediterraneans into this ocean, Slanning, and there'd not be noticed even a rise of tide! And heed ye, on the other side of Darien there's another ocean I have heard is even vaster than this one. That is the Southern Sea, which has been named the Pacific."

He lowered his voice, as though he'd named a secret.

"I tell you, Slanning, some day you and I will look out upon that sea. Aye, and sail it! For why should the Spaniards have it to themselves? Do they own the earth?"

"They think they do."

"They'll learn better, sirrah. Did God Almighty create all that water, too, only for their benefit?"

So they would talk whilst resting between bouts; and those hours in the waist, fencing and talking, were the happiest Talbot spent aboard the *Pascha*. For it was then that he felt himself a useful part of the ship. At other times he was humbled by the clean efficiency, the sureness and confidence of the mariners; he was made to seem awkward, ignorant, unwanted. But in the waist it was different, for there he was himself superior; and besides, the exercise customarily loosened the Captain's tongue.

"So you think like the others that galleys filled with soldiers, in whatsoever sea, can whip such lumbering vessels as this one? Where would they store food for all those oarsmen? They can go fast, aye, but only when the sea's a lake. And where would they base? They can never venture more than a few miles from any port."

They were seated side by side on the waist hatch, and the Captain absently slapped his slippered foot with his rapier.

"A month ago I would have laughed if any man told me that a fellow with only a splinter of steel, and not once cutting with the edge, could make Francis Drake, the best sword-and-buckler fighter in Tavistock, look like a clumsy housewife stumbling over her broom. And still I cannot understand it, quite. I don't know how it's done. But I know it *is* done! I grant that you have greater knowledge of the sword then me, but it never would have been possible for you to convince me with arguments whilst we were seated like this. Nay, I must see it happen! I must feel myself slash air, and feel myself trip! I must feel the prod fairly against my ribs, making me grunt! *Then* I believe that in truth you know whereof you talk, eh? Can you not understand that this is so too with ships?"

He rose.

"And now, will you show me again, pray, that *guardia largha in sotto*? Surely with the right foot forward that leaves the breast unprotected? Should I have advance my dagger just enough to . . ."

On the twenty-third day, while Talbot was taking a siesta—a habit new but most naturally formed—they raised Dominica. Somebody waked him, and he took a bleary look.

It was not exciting, he thought. Fabulous America? It was nothing more than a blurred, blue-gray thickening of the horizon. It might have been France. Or Essex.

They coasted until they discovered a small rocky island where there was a spring, and there they remained for three days, stretching their legs, filling their casks, stocking up with firewood, fishing. It was a bleak, hot, flea-bitten place. "Not like Devonshire," Robert Butterwalk remarked.

It was here that Talbot had his first sight of the Spaniards of the New World.

Some hours later a crank-sided carrack, obviously no fighter, and none too trimly rigged, approached them with confidence. Captain Drake would have permitted her to pass without hail, for he had no desire to have the Spaniards learn that he was in this part of the world, but she came on. She dropped anchor; she sent to the *Pascha* a cockboat containing four oarsmen and a beplumed, beribboned grandee.

Halfway, this boat stopped; the grandee looked doubtful, having noted the muzzles of guns; but Captain Drake roared in broken Spanish:

"Nay, since you've come this far, come aboard!"

The grandee had no choice but to obey.

He was Don Alvarez de Ruidiaz, commanding the *San Antonio*, out of Cartagena for Seville, loaded with cochineal, cinnamon, a few casks of small pearls, and many tons of water from a supposedly health-giving spring. This cargo was not important—Captain Drake would not touch such trifles. What mattered was the fact that Don Alvarez instantly recognized the Englishman.

"Señor el Capitan Drake! El Draque!"

They knew him, these Spaniards, and respected him, as Talbot was to learn. Don Alvarez, though supposing that he was about to lose both ship and cargo, protested —and he probably meant it, too—that he was overwhelmed by the honor of meeting El Draque again.

El Draque, the Spaniards called him: The Dragon.

These two commanders had a talk, with the help of Talbot Slanning, whose Spanish was coming back to him in great gusts. When Don Alvarez learned that he would not be robbed, he gladly agreed to continue his course to Seville and not to put back to the New World with a warning that El Draque was again on the Main. After that Captain Drake breathed easier.

Nevertheless Captain Drake remained on deck for a long while that afternoon, watching the carrack get smaller and smaller, and Talbot heard him mutter, "Eh, and I hope that fine fellow didn't lie to me. We'll take no risk of it. Tomorrow we'll up anchor."

Their second landfall was at Sierra Nevada, behind Santa Marta. The Captain had discovered a secret harbor there the previous year, and had buried a supply of gunpowder and provisions. Port Pheasant, he'd named it. It was a fine round bay between two high points, eight or ten cable-lengths across, but not more than half a cable-length at the mouth. A perfect hiding place, with ten to twelve fathoms of water, a gently tilted beach, a jungle packed with fruits of all sorts, plenty of fish, game, water, wood.

It was here that the Captain explained at last to his brother, to Talbot and Robert, Hixom and Oxenham, and to Tom Moone, the master gunner, where he meant to go and what he meant to do.

It left them breathless.

There was a map, a stiff yellow thing which the Captain took with great care from a sea chest. He cleared his throat.

"We seek great treasure," he started abruptly. "Greater treasure than is contained in all England."

Imperiously he pointed to the map. He might have been Alexander of Macedon alloting satrapies to favored dependants.

"Twice each year two *flotas* set forth from Seville to fetch for King Philip the wealth that his colonies have amassed. One is the *flota* of New Spain, which the natives call Mexico. The other is the *flota* of Tierra Firma. They sail together as far as Hispaniola, their landfall, and then one goes to San Juan de Ulua, the other to Cartegena, the capital of the Main. This second fleet, after loading at Cartegena, proceeds to a small city on the coast of Darien called Nombre de Dios. Mark Nombre de Dios well, gentlemen. It is there that this fleet picks up the treasures coasted up the shores of the Southern Sea from Peruana, where no white men save Spaniards ever have been, to the city of Panama, from whence it is carried by *recuas*, or mule trains, across the Isthmus to Nombre de Dios.

"Thereafter this *flota* proceeds up through the Yucatan Channel and makes contact with the *flota* of New Spain at Habana-de-Cuba. Together they sail north through the New Bahamas Channel and thence east to the Azores and Seville. But they no longer go unescorted! The Indian Guard of twelve stout fighting galleons is with them. And for this reason they are too strong to be touched.

"However, there is a time before the Peruana treasure is loaded into these vessels—a few days when it is kept in vaults at Nombre de Dios waiting for the arrival of the *flota* from Cartegena. For this Isthmus of Panama, Darien, is the bottleneck through which half the wealth of the world passes each year."

He rolled the map, tied it with tape, and replaced it.

"We sack Nombre de Dios, gentlemen," he announced simply. "And now be about your tasks."

He was not asking their opinion: he was telling them his. He assumed that they would follow him blindly.

They sat stunned, aghast of the boldness of the plan. And as they sat there, hot in the little stuffy cabin, a call came from the lookout above:

"Sail, ho! Sail, ho!"

There was no scramble of excitement. The Captain looked for and found his brass glass, and without haste he went on deck; and the others followed him.

There were three vessels. One, by far the largest, loafed in the offing. It was a tall ship and somewhat resembled the *Pascha*. A shallop preceded it, and before the shallop was a small caravel. The smaller vessels were propelled by sweeps.

"The ship might be almost anything," remarked Captain Drake, "but the coasters are Spanish. That's sure."

He turned to Robert Butterwalk.

"Ashore, please, and dispatch men to each of the points with word that the demi-culverins are to be fired if and when I loose a pennant from the outrigger."

He turned to Talbot.

"Below, please, and tell Tom Moone to open all cannon ports and send up powder for each deck. Have the sakers and fowlers brought here, with ball and powder, and the bases mounted starboard on the afterdeck."

He raised the glass and resumed his study of the newcomers.

They came slowly, as though uncertain of what manner of reception awaited them. It was not likely that they had spotted the shore batteries. Once beyond the point, whether or not their commander knew it, they were trapped.

The shallop moved close, and somebody called: "Ahoy! Who in the name of a pig's arse hole are *you?*"

Drake nodded thoughtfully.

"English," he murmured.

He cupped his hands to his mouth.

"Captain Francis Drake with *Pascha* and *Swan* out of Plymouth. Who's your admiral?"

The answer came: "Captain James Ranse in *Griffen*, out of the Wight. And two Spanish prizes."

"A scamp," Drake muttered, half to himself. "I know him. A Channel pirate. But we'll have to take him into the venture or his presence in this part of the world would spoil everything."

And he shouted: "Send Captain Ranse to me."

While they waited for the shallop to take this message

63

to the ship Captain Drake conferred with his brother Joseph and with Hixom. The *Griffen*, it was learned, was a one-hundred-and-ten-ton vessel, formerly a Dutcher, now owned by Sir Edward Horsey, governor of the Isle of Wight, who evidently was branching out. Ranse, Drake said, had sailed for various English owners, and also for the Huguenots and for the Low Country rebels. A skillful mariner, but a shifty, unreliable man.

"Three times while we were preparing he came to me with the suggestion that I make this same *Griffen* a part of my fleet, and himself second-in-command. But I refused. I don't like him."

Hixom offered: " 'Tis said he hath great influence over Horsey. Maybe he persuaded the governor to permit this voyage after all."

"Likely. And spoil it for us. Regard those two cockle-shells that he's plucked. And the alarm will be out."

Ranse was a tall dark man of good breeding and some education, but given to a pose of roughness: he was a hand pumper, a back slapper, embarrassingly hearty.

"Well met, Frank! When did you sail out of Plymouth, eh? I quit the Wight on the 23rd of last month. Twenty-seven days to Martinique! Such a wind I never did know! And a fine sailer I've got there. But what's about? I've forty-three stout fellows, ready and glad to slice a Spanish throat or two if the plan calls for such, as I'll warrant it does, eh? Tell me about it, and we'll throw in together."

Captain Drake nodded a glum head.

"I have a project, aye. Come to my cabin and I'll recite it. But I think 'twould be well to have here also your second and third in command, eh?"

"The one's mastering it aboard the shallop, the other aboard the caravel. I'll have 'em here in a scoop of moments."

He leaned over the rail and gave orders to the boatmen. Then he linked his arm with Captain Drake's.

"Oho! That us two old sea dogs should meet in this hole forsaken of God! Methinks that calls for wine, eh, Frank?"

"It might be well," Captain Drake suggested, "if we two old sea dogs fall down on our knees first and give thanks to the Almighty for bringing us both here alive and in sound health."

The visitor looked startled, then laughed.

"Aye, a right good proposal, Frank! But the wine first, eh? We'll wait the prayers till the others join us. I never could be very pious when I was thirsty."

Nobody followed them. Nobody aboard the *Pascha* ever went into Captain's cabin without his permission.

Joseph Drake and the other officers, like the Captain himself, seemed none too happy about the appearance of Ranse. But Robert Butterwalk, ashore, and Talbot Slanning, aboard, were elated, excited, thrilled at the prospect of meeting fellow countrymen after having supposed, humanly enough, that except for the two ships' companies there were no other Englishmen within three thousand miles of this quiet bay.

The officers lingered at the head of the ladder, awaiting the arrival of Ranse's second and third in command. Joseph Drake was to receive them for his brother. But Talbot hurried below to his own quarters in order to don a clean ruff and to strap on his sword, for assuredly this would be a ceremonious occasion.

A few minutes later, a trifle out of breath, he hurried back on deck just in time to see Tom Gillard step off the ladder.

CHAPTER EIGHT

If Gillard felt an amazement in any way comparable to Talbot's, it did not show in his large dark face. He looked angry, sullen; but that was his usual appearance. His mouth did not fall open, nor was there any change in his purplish-blue, venomous eyes. He might have been encountering his enemy in the streets of Chagford instead of a hidden harbor on the other side of the world.

"Ah! The messenger boy again," was all he said.

Talbot could not have been so astounded if he were faced by a ghost. He stood motionless except for his right hand, which had been engaged in fastening the belt buckle and still fumbled with that buckle absently, unthinkingly.

"Belting?" Tom Gillard asked. "Or unbelting?"

This could not be the deck of a ship in a tropic bay. This was not Darien, it was Devonshire. It was the room upstairs at the Three Crowns.

"*Un*belting, I make no doubt? Aye. 'Twould be safer."

The others gawped; for though they were acquainted with Talbot's story, none had recognized Tom Gillard, so none understood the strange behavior of these two. Robert Butterwalk would have known; but he was ashore.

Wrath poured into Talbot Slanning. The blood suddenly seemed to leave his head, so that his face went cold. He must have looked pale. Perhaps he looked afraid?

"Nay, belting," he cried.

He snapped the buckle tongue into the last hole.

"*Belting*, so that we can finish our engagement!"

He whipped out sword and dagger.

"Draw, sir!"

Gillard drew without the slightest hesitation.

This time neither man gave ground. Talbot was cut twice above the right ear, but those were glancing blows and at the time he did not even feel them. He sacrificed his head guard to lunge full length for Gillard's heart. Gillard twisted, and the thrust only ripped open his doublet.

Then somebody back by the Captain's cabin gave a great shout, and big Tom Moone leapt forward to throw his arms around Talbot's chest. At the same time a hoop of rope was thrown over Gillard's head, and he was jerked with a crash to the deck.

Talbot too was down, and the fall stunned him. He struggled to get to his feet, but Tom Moone was half atop him and still holding his arms.

Then Captain Drake was there, with Captain Ranse. Ranse looked excited, but Drake was ice.

"I know not how you deal with brawlers," he told Ranse, "but for myself, I shackle 'em till they cool."

He looked at Talbot as though he did not recognize him, as though here was some obnoxious stranger.

"Put him in irons," he told Tom Moone.

For five days Talbot Slanning remained in a dim room below decks. He had entered that room a fiery and thoughtless youth, but he was to emerge a man.

He was given plenty to eat and drink, and Tom Moone, his jailor, permitted him to walk on the deck twice a day. There were both leg irons and wrist irons in his prison, but while he was being taken there a mariner had come with word from the Captain revoking the order to use these irons: clearly that order had been made for show purposes: Ranse must be impressed.

Moreover, Talbot was told that he would be immediately reinstated whenever he gave his promise to refrain from private fighting while this adventure endured.

"He says that afterward you can do whatever you wish to Ranse's lieutenant, but that whilst you're on Francis Drake's ship you must obey Francis Drake's orders."

"Tell Francis Drake," Talbot had snarled, "that he is dealing with a man of gentle blood, not some damned mariner."

And Tom Moone had shrugged and departed. He liked Master Slanning, but he adored Captain Drake. He thought that here Master Slanning was playing the fool.

In this Tom was correct, as Talbot himself came to realize. For Talbot was exercising a young man's privilege of being hotheaded and stubborn. This was being burned out of him; and the process, though but mental, was acute. He did suffer.

He refused to take the daily exercise walk permitted him, being damned, he said, if he would toddle before the gaze of officers and hands, a man to be stared at, snickered at. He knew the passing of time only by the clang of the ship's bells, and after a while, because of sleep, he lost track of these, and did not even know when it was night and when it was day. Nor did he care, he told himself.

Not many hours after he had been imprisoned he felt the *Pascha* move. Soon he could tell from the gentle roll that she was in the open sea again, outside. He wondered whether that meant that they were headed for Nombre de Dios.

Twice each day Tom Moone recited: "The Captain's respects, and he wishes to know if you are ready to promise not to brawl whilst sailing on this ship?"

"My compliments to the Captain and tell him to go to the Devil."

At first he was hot, then for some time cold, bitter. And then one day, unexpectedly, amazing even himself, he commenced to laugh.

Francis Drake was right, of course. Francis Drake was always right about matters nautical. There would be a day to fight Tom Gillard. There was other work to be done first.

The next time Tom Moone repeated his formula Talbot rose.

"Take me to the Captain, please."

Nobody stared as Talbot followed Tom across the deck. Even the hands tried to act as though nothing had happened, and perhaps they too were embarrassed. Nevertheless Talbot Slanning blushed. It was a difficult thing to do, what he was about to do.

The Captain was genial, even solicitous. He poured Talbot a cup of canary, inquired concerning his health, was assured that he had been well treated.

"You were right and I was wrong," Talbot said. "I'll not fight a personal fight whilst I serve under your command."

The Captain waved a deprecating hand.

"There'll be plenty of the other kind to do," he said.

They swallowed wine, each seeking a different topic of conversation.

"Where are we?" Talbot asked. "We've been sailing."

The ship was motionless then, anchored off a cluster of fir-covered islands.

Drake nodded in the direction of the shore.

"These are the Islas de Pinos, about twenty-five leagues

east of Nombre de Dios. The three ships and the caravel are to be left here, with Captain Ranse, and I will take the pinnaces and the shallop. They're smaller and faster. Ranse and I have signed articles of temporary partnership. He remains in charge of the rear guard, but I will take twenty of his men, in command of your friend Master Gillard, together with fifty-three of my own men. We sail in a few hours."

Talbot did not ask the question he was burning to ask. Notwithstanding, Francis Drake answered it.

"I should admire to have you go with us," he said.

"I shall be proud to do so," Talbot said.

Somehow they were better friends from that time on. They had previously trusted and respected one another, but now they seemed to understand one another as well.

The Captain finished his wine.

"There is another matter," he said slowly.

Talbot was watching him.

"Here at Islas de Pinos we came upon some of the Maroons. Have you heard of these same Maroons?"

Talbot shook his head.

"They were slaves, black men from Africa, but of a hardy fighting stock. They escaped from the Spaniards and took to the hills, attacked some of the Indians and stole their women, and now they are divided into powerful tribes. They prey upon the colonists like wild beasts—and are treated as such when they're caught. They have been living in the hills for some eighty years, and they hate the Spaniards more than anything else on this earth. The dons call them Cimaroons, or hill people. Maroons."

"Can we trust them?"

"I think so. I did them some favors when I was there before, and I picked up a few words of their gibberish.

70

From what I can learn, the garrison at Nombre de Dios has been recently reinforced."

"They've learned that we have come?"

"No, they did not suspect our presence. The Maroons have been especially bold of late, and it is against them that the dons are preparing. And best I could make out from what these Maroons said, the treasure fleet is there, the royal *recuas* have all come from Panama, and we must act quickly. This is as I knew it would be. But I did not know that the savages would cause such consternation at Nombre de Dios that the inhabitants there would construct a battery on the hill on the east side of the bay. Nor did I expect to find one hundred and fifty royal Spanish troops there from Panama.

The Captain turned his wine cup around and around.

"Of course this will not cause me to change my plans. I did not come half way across the world to be turned aside by a hundred and fifty Spanish soldiers and a few bits of brass."

The Maroons, he went on, could not get in or even near Nombre de Dios. Every soldier and even every civilian was under orders to shoot them on sight. Those ashore here at Islas de Pinos were willing to try a reconnoitering trip; but there was not time for this.

"Still I should like to know whether that battery has been placed and properly manned, and where the reinforcements have been quartered. I should also like to know whether the treasures brought from Panama are stored in the Governor's house or in the Cabildo, which is what they call their town hall, you understand, Slanning."

"Please go on."

"If there was one of my own men there, to meet me when we launch the attack, and to give me this information—"

Talbot was on his feet.

"*Do they know the path?*"

"There's no path, only jungle. But they do know that, aye. But understand me well," the Captain said, and he spoke slowly, carefully, looking hard at Talbot. "I do not command this. I do not even ask it. Should you refuse, you'd still receive your share of any adventurers' profits in this enterprise."

"I'll go!"

"We could land you near the mouth of the Rio Francisco and the Maroons could guide you to the town gates, which you might reach by Wednesday, if you started now. Thursday morning, at dawn, the attack will be launched from the shore near the customs-house dock."

He went to a cabinet, took out a steel morion, a set of backplates, a heavily ridged breastplate with a tapul in the Spanish style.

"Your sword and dagger are from Madrid anyway. Your face has been darkened by the sun. You speak Spanish. With the fleet in from Cartegena, Nombre de Dios will be crowded with strange mariners and gentlemen. Best of all, no one will dream that there's a single Englishman on this side of the Atlantic Ocean."

"A badge—a cognizance?"

"Your shirt, wrapped and tied around your left arm. This only in the hour before we descend upon the city. Each one of us will wear his own shirt the same way."

He came close to Talbot, touched Talbot's arm in a tender way.

"Please believe me, I do not command this. 'Tis a task fraught with uncertainty. If you're caught, Slanning, it will mean not merely death but a long and horrible torture."

Talbot took off his bonnet and clapped on the morion, the steel headpiece. He picked up the backplates.

"Where do I meet these Maroons?" he asked.

Sunlight stunned and stung him. It was like the blast of bright white heat when the door of a furnace is flung open. Literally, he staggered. He might have been a man struck on the chest.

For seventeen or eighteen hours, as nearly as he could reckon, he had been slogging through swamp and jungle, an underworld so dark as to seem solid shadow, into which light could not penetrate. It had been Hell. In a welter of weariness, wet, muddy, his hose slashed by spiked vines, his face and hands puffed with the bites of insects, he had somehow come through. But he could scarcely stand; and when he stumbled out into a sun-drenched clearing the wonder was that he wasn't stricken blind.

He had been accompanied by phantoms, an unnerving experience. He did not even know how many of the Maroons there were. They were tall, extraordinarily strong, and as lithe as cats. They wore no clothes and carried no weapons. Each had hung from his neck a carved and painted bull's horn or ox's horn, and in this he kept dried corn, which when mixed with spring water was his provender; but Talbot never did see any of them eat. Nor did they ever speak to him, though they smiled and sometimes waved. He seldom glimpsed them at all, and when he did it was in the form of flashing teeth or smiling rolling eyes; but he always knew that they were there. When he would flump upon the ground in some relatively dry spot, to rest a while, the Maroons would cluster around him, and squat, watching him like birds. They themselves, he gathered, might have gone on forever.

They had mothered and guided him, surrounding him like a swarm of benevolent bees. He was going to Nombre de Dios for the purpose of killing Spaniards, they had been told, and killing Spaniards they esteemed a matter of supreme importance. They were still there in the jungle behind him, he assumed, though he could not see a one.

He couldn't see much of anything, at first. But when his eyes had adjusted themselves to the brilliance he perceived that he was indeed in a sort of large clearing, or perhaps it could be better called the edge of the jungle. On his right were hills, but on his left the ground fell sharply away and he could glimpse in the distance—and a heartlifting sight it was!—the bright blue sea. Ahead of him was the trace of a path, no more. No smoke stood up in the sky, nor could he hear the sound of any bell, yet the conviction grew in him, as he stood there swaying, that he was close to civilization again. Somehow he *sensed* it.

The Maroons behind him might have sensed the same thing, or known of it. They did not appear. "This," they seemed to be trying to say to him—though still he could not see or hear them—"this is as far as we can go. The rest is up to you." What lay immediately before him, Talbot divined, was a sort of *terra damnata* or no-man's-land, a buffer zone established between these implacable enemies, one in which neither could consider himself safe, it being not hills and not yet the town.

He drew, tremblingly, a deep breath. The air was damp and hot, as the air of the jungle had been. Any exertion, however slight, made a man pant.

He was hungry, he was thirsty, but above all he was weary. He had been frightened too, back there. In the blazing sunshine he admitted to himself with a blush that a few times he had been on the very verge of panic. But now he was too tired to care. Had he permitted his instincts to tell him how to act he would simply have

74

dropped to the ground, armor and all, for a long, long sleep. But if he did that he might be found by some Spanish patrol and asked to explain himself before he could clear his wits. He could be killed or at least seriously addled by the sun itself, a murderous enemy in this part of the world. Besides, he did not know what kind of wild beasts might lurk in these parts. Surely there would be poisonous reptiles. From time to time as he floundered through the swamp Talbot had seen reddish glowing eyes low against the slime and had heard a heavy slick scraping sound, followed by a splash, as some huge unseen saurian slipped away. But they might not slip away if they found him asleep.

No, he must keep his feet at all costs.

He worked off his morion. The strap all but took away skin from his chin. The thing was pitilessly hot and heavy, as were the back and breastplates he wore, possibly the most impractical attire for a jungle jaunt that ever man had designed; but Talbot had found it less tiring to wear than to carry. Now he stared at the inside of the helmet. He thought of seeking water for washing purposes, using the morion as a basin; but for this moment he was too dazed to think or even to move.

He heard a step, and looked up.

A man had entered the clearing from the far end and was trotting toward Talbot. He was a Spaniard, small, not young. Like Talbot he was torn and splattered; yet he ran, somehow; and his mouth was opened in a glad cry to greet Talbot.

It was a cry he never was to deliver.

He must have come from Nombre de Dios or from one of the mule trains along the Panama Trail. He had strayed, got lost, and spent a terrifying time in the jungle. His joy at the sight of Talbot—who with his Spanish armor represented home, safety—was touching.

How should Talbot salute him? What story to give? Talbot was not prepared for such an encounter, having supposed that he'd be allowed a little time in which to study the situation outside of the gates of Nombre de Dios. In so far as he had a plan, it was to remain aloof, disdainful, playing the part of some poor but ineffably proud minor grandee. This would spare him casual conversation, he hoped. For he was not sure of his Spanish —schoolbooky stuff plus what he had picked up in the shops and fencing academies of Madrid, and not ably lacking the cant of mariners and colonial adventurers.

He paused, irresolute.

He was not given time to decide what to do. Out of the great wet green-black wall of foliage behind him suddenly the Maroons came leaping. They gave no war cries, and made no sound of any sort, but they closed with incredible speed upon the luckless man in the clearing.

That man saw them for a horrid instant. His face showed such an expression as Talbot never hoped to see again. He screamed.

Then Talbot saw him no more, for the blacks had him on the ground.

Some clubbed with their horns. Others used the points of these to stab. Many simply tore with their hands.

It was quickly over. The scream was cut off, nor was there any echo of it or any following moan. There were five of the Maroons, and they literally ripped that poor little Spaniard to pieces.

Talbot too might have screamed: he wasn't sure. He dropped the morion and ran to the surging seething black group, where he grabbed arms and shoulders, slapping and slamming his way to the figure on the ground.

The Maroons made no resistance. They even seemed

pleased, and fell back with gleeful, see-what-a-brave-boy-am-I grins.

The Spaniard was dead. That much at least was certain. The heart had stopped; and other details, gruesome enough, were not significent. He lay on his back, his sleazy clothes torn off, his head and crotch bulging pulpy masses of blood and shredded flesh around which already the flies were gathering. Both of his eyes had been gouged out. All his teeth were gone, and the mouth was lacerated beyond recognition. The testicles had been hacked away, and one of the Maroons held these on high, beaming with delight. But the heart *had* stopped. Of that much at least Talbot made sure.

If Talbot had had anything on his stomach he might have been sick, though he was by no means a squeemish man. He did not trust himself to look at the Maroons except to verify by means of signs the direction of Nombre de Dios. This might have wounded their feelings, for they thought that they had done something fine. The one who held the testacles kept waggling these as though they were a couple of earrings he was trying to sell in some Oriental market.

Buzzards, not so swift as the flies, but yet uncannily prompt, were coming over the hill, flying lumbrously and low. They had smelled blood.

This in less than a minute—in seconds.

Talbot recovered his helmet, and he left that place.

He looked back only once. The Maroons, no doubt fearing that buzzards might attract the attention of Spaniards farther away, were dragging their corpse into the jungle. They waved to Talbot, and then they vanished, body and all. And he heard a dull splash. Some alligator would do a quicker job then the buzzards could, and leave less mess.

Despite the heat, Talbot shivered.

The path, faint at first, became clearer. The Spanish wretch, if he had but turned the other way, by this time would have been safe at home; for Talbot had no trouble making his way to the Panama Trail.

It was not an imposing thoroughfare, not paved in any way, a grubby, meandering lane, cut by the hoofs and strewn with the droppings of many mules, though at the moment there was neither man nor beast in sight.

The sun was high, nearing noon, yet Talbot was not sure of his directions, and he waited for a little while.

A train of eight mules went by, laden with some exotic fruit. There were two goaders, and they both nodded to Talbot, one of them lifting a floppy straw hat.

Four impassive Indians came next, walking stolidly in single file, on the head of each a great shapeless bundle. Behind them strode a man in a blue coat, who carried a whip.

Talbot strolled after this second party, being careful not to catch up with it.

It was in this way that he came to the south gate, the Panama Trail gate, of Nombre de Dios. This was a mean stingy opening in a fifteen-foot mud wall, and it was guarded only by a pikeman, with whom at the time of Talbot's arrival the man in the blue coat was noisily arguing, while the four Indians, as patient as water buffalos, stood on one side.

Talbot Slanning did not pause. He simply walked past the sentry, not even troubling to give a nod. The sentry glanced at him but did not challenge.

Talbot was in Nombre de Dios.

He was in the midst of the enemy.

CHAPTER NINE

Beyond all doubt, he knew right away, the fleet was in. Nombre de Dios ordinarily would have been a tiny, hot, flea-bitten place, but this afternoon it was not, at least, somnolent; for it was crowded with mariners. Talbot did not scurry, but neither did he saunter. He talked to no one, and acknowledged no hail, but he kept his ears and eyes open, and very soon he had sought out and found a place where he could wash.

After that he made for a wineshop.

"Señor?"

He did not stew, but demanded, unhesitatingly, Ribadavia.

"And," he added, "food."

"Sí, señor."

To his astonishment he got the Ribadavia, and it was good, so good indeed that he decided he should sip it slowly, meanwhile eating as much as he could manage to eat. The food too, was good, if you liked Spanish food. It was very spicy, and seemed to be based on some sort of white meat which wasn't a fish. There was a great deal of it.

Talbot nodded in grudging approval. The place was

crowded; and he ate slowly, and sipped the wine as though it stabbed his lips. He would loiter and listen.

If he listens carefully enough, a man can learn a great deal while he eats.

This much he took in without effort:

That the plate fleet was from Cartegena and would sail in two days or possibly three days.

That the treasure from Panama was indeed stored in the Cabildo and in the Governor's house; though which of these structures was the stronger and which contained the more wealth he could not make out.

That the reinforcements had been quartered with the regular garrison in a long, low wooden barracks near the Panama gate.

That the battery on the east hill had been mounted but not yet manned, only two caretakers being stationed there, each armed with a musketoon intended to serve less as a weapon of defense than as an instrument of warning in case of alarm.

That the town seethed with talk about the recent raid of the Maroons, which had very nearly taken it, and the chance of another such attack.

All of this Talbot overheard and digested, even while he was eating. There could be no secrets here in Nombre de Dios, since there could be but one enemy—the naked, savage, illiterate, and wholly unpredictable Maroons.

Sometimes there would be a passing reference to French corsairs; but nobody ever mentioned the English.

Talbot nodded, and belched, and finished his meal. He paid, went to the jakes, and then went outdoors for an examination of the town.

He was in no hurry. It was barely noon.

Once again, it did not take him long to learn what he

had come to learn. This assignment, so far, was too easy to be true.

Now and then, as he walked about, somebody would speak to him; but all he did, each time, was shake his head and go on.

Nombre de Dios was square, perhaps two miles on each side, and consisted of one avenue and a dozen-odd unimportant side streets. The avenue extended from the beach, at a point near the customhouse, generally upward and south to the Panama Trail gate. Two-thirds of the way up to that gate was the Plaza, the center of Nombre de Dios. Halfway up the grade between the beach and the Plaza, on the right as you went down, was the town hall, a grimly strong-looking building.

There were no interior fortifications, the garrison was grouped at the back of the town, the south, near the Panama gate, and the beach was unprotected except by a battery of four small brass cannons which could have been put there only for display purposes or as saluters. It was because the Maroons had no sort of boats, Talbot supposed, that the beach was left open. The other three sides, the land sides of the town, were lined with mud walls on top of which temporary wooden boardings had been erected. These walls were well posted.

It was only the Maroons that Nombre de Dios feared. Attack from the sea side could come as an utter surprise.

One other building only did Talbot Slanning take note of, and that was on a side street. It was demure, having no sign before it; but its function was apparent from the men who came and left. It might as *well* have had a sign: *Casa de Diversión*, say, or *Casa Pública*, or, more outspokenly, *bordello*. In itself, as an institution at this outpost, it spoke well for Spanish colonial thought. They were realists, those dons! When the great Fernando Alvarez de Toledo, Duke of Alva, had been

81

sent forth to quell the rebellion in the Low Countries with the greatest fighting force Europe ever had known, did he not have, along with his ten thousand magnificently equipped and rigorously trained soldiers, *two thousand* accomplished, experienced prostitutes, each holding a registration card? There were troopers in Nombre de Dios too, if not so many; and why should they be neglected?

The house had a meek aspect. Yet men, even Spaniards, habitually approached and left such an establishment furtively. Might it not be a good place in which to sleep?

Talbot thought only of sleeping then. He did not suppose that he could stand on his feet much longer.

And he had Spanish coins in his pocket. This too had been arranged. He must have been rich, as local standards went.

The women would be fresh from the home country, he reasoned, and recently tested, not holding disease.

But . . . the fleet was in. This *casa de diversión* would be busy. Whores do not relish men who sleep on the premises when there are many mariners lately paid.

Talbot sighed; he went back to the wineship, where he ordered another jack of Ribadavia.

He reconsidered the situation. He did this as he drank the wine in part to help himself stay awake. Sleep might prove the biggest problem of all. Drake was not due until dawn, and it was not yet dark. Unless Talbot found some place to sleep in the meanwhile he would be of no use to his captain and indeed might not even be conscious at the time of the attack. There was no inn at Nombre de Dios. The soldiers slept in their barracks, the sailors aboard their respective vessels. The regular residents, the well-to-do and their servants, slept in houses. Casual, unattached visitors of lowly origin, such as mule drivers from Panama, Talbot gathered, simply curled up in their

82

blankets on the beach, or else under one of the arcades that faced the Plaza; but it would never do for an *hidalgo* in body armor to be found sleeping out-of-doors.

So Talbot drank and thought, as before keeping his ears cocked.

The beach was virtually unguarded. The customhouse itself had nothing fortlike about it: the walls were of stone but not notably strong and not pierced with slits for crossbow or musket fire. Given luck and a dark night a skilled mariner should be able to bring three pinnaces and a shallop around the west point of the bay before these were seen. And even when they were seen it was unlikely that there would be an alarm, for all sorts of coasting vessels were converging upon Nombre de Dios at this season of the *flota*, and in fact the shallop at least *was* such a vessel.

The chances for a surprise, then, were excellent.

The reinforcements, as the Maroons had reported, numbered one hundred and fifty. The regular garrison consisted of eighty men, including officers. Fifteen professional soldiers invariably accompanied every royal *recua* from Panama, and Talbot gathered that at least eight or nine of these had recently arrived, in addition to certain private *recuas*, which also would be escorted by soldiers. It was reasonable to suppose that many of these lingered in the town to enjoy the bustle of loading or perhaps to help fleece the mariners. In addition, many, probably most of the male citizens of Nombre de Dios were armed, and though disorganized could be counted upon to fight for the defense of the town.

Francis Drake would have seventy-three men, including himself. If he was not met by Talbot with news that the battery on the east hill was not manned and so could not be used to cut off his retreat—if he had to send a

83

detachment out there, beyond the town walls—then surely he would be lost, wiped out.

Talbot lingered in the wineshop. Not that he liked the place; but it seemed safe, it was filled with loose-tongued drinkers, and he himself was inconspicuous here. Moreover he had learned that it was something in the nature of a hostel. There were several private rooms upstairs, all rented now, as well as one large common room to which those who got drunk downstairs were led or carried for sleep. There were places of the same sort in Plymouth and London, and indeed Talbot assumed that it was a common water front practice. It pleased the civic authorities, for it helped to keep the drunken seamen off the streets. It pleased the ships' officers, who knew where to go when men were missing. And of course it pleased the proprietor of the wineship, who could steal a coin or two on occasion.

That public sleeping-it-off place, Talbot reflected, might be convenient. He ordered another jack of Ribadavia.

A sly, rat-faced little fellow chattered pauselessly at Talbot's elbow, and it was with something of a start that Talbot learned he was talking to *him*.

"Uh, what was that again?"

"I said my master, *señor*, my gracious master, the illustrious Don Ernesto Jesus de Santillana y Canovia, hath engaged one of the private rooms, and do you know for what?"

Talbot hiccoughed, and took a drink of wine. The rat-faced man, seeming to suppose that this implied interest in his talk, answered his own question.

"He prays again to the blessed Virgin Mary, *señor*, for the strength to live until he can arrange to have himself transferred to England in the suite of the King's ambassador."

Now Talbot observed that his companion wore a blue

coat, and on the left sleeve was sewn a cognizance: sable, a fess wavy between two axes argent, undoubtedly the arms of the illustrious Don Ernesto.

"And d'ye know *why* he wishes to go to England?"

Talbot hiccoughed again, and managed a bleary nod. Evidently Ratface was almost as drunk as he himself pretended to be.

"Why, 'tis for that he hath sworn a great vow that the heretic queen, Lisbet, shall be killed by his own hand. Eh, I tell you my master's a pious man! For hath not this Lisbet wilfully been quit of Mother Church, and hath not the Holy Father at Rome issued a bull of deposition against her? And so, my master thinks, that the son of the Church who thrusts a dagger into her heart, him will the angels love."

Ratface chuckled, and took a deep drink of wine, Talbot's.

Talbot staggered to his feet, turned in the direction of the stairway. He put a hand upon Ratface's shoulder, as though to steady himself; but the servant mistook this for a friendly slap, and he rose, all eagerness.

"Would you ascend and have a peek at my illustrious master, eh, *señor?*"

Talbot nodded.

"Aye, show me him."

CHAPTER TEN

It was not because of any burning desire to see Don Ernesto Jesus that Talbot decided to go upstairs. It was because he wished to have a look at the common sleeping room.

This was on the right. It was without candles, though a drizzle of starlight struggled between the bars at the window and fell to the dirty bare floor. Only two figures were stretched out on that floor, and both snored boisterously. There was not a scrap of furniture, not so much as a mat.

Ratface opened a door across the hall, peeked in, then beckoned to Talbot, bidding him come. He had all the excited pride of a mother who displays to a guest her cradled sleeping child.

"He will pray like this all the night through, *señor*. He seems a weak man, except when he prays, and then he has the strength of great faith. He has taken the vow, and now he prays that he will be enabled to fulfill it."

Talbot peered in.

The illustrious Don Ernesto Jesus de Santillana y Canovia was on his knees, his back to the door. He faced a brightly painted Madonna about twelve inches tall, flanked by lighted candles. His head was low in humility, but his back was a ramrod. That back alone might have stamped him a Castilian; for it was eloquent of pride, of ancient and outworn but still-cherished convictions of grandeur. They could not see the face; but the back of the head and the back of the neck were cruelly, un-healthily thin.

The man was mumbling. His voice seemed that of somebody else, a thing apart from him, unreal. The voice crept around the room like an eerie unsubstantial creature from another world: it shuddered among the shadows, a restless malevolent sprite, agonized, unable to be still.

The sight was one Talbot never was able to erase from his memory.

This Spanish gentlemen had sworn to assassinate or to arrange the assassination of Elizabeth of England. In some minds it would be, as Ratface had pointed out, an act of patriotism and a guarantee of eternal bliss after death. It would mean a bloody civil war, the squashing of the Church of England, possibly union with Spain and after that still further war with France, and certainly the end to all the dreams of such men as Francis Drake. Talbot, peeking, could hear the little redhead splutter between fencing bouts in the waist of the *Pascha*: "They'd crowd us off the earth, if they were able to! Aye, and they'll make the effort, unless we strike first!" But Talbot was thinking less of Francis Drake and his dreams of empire than of the danger to the Queen herself. Somehow she seemed very real and near to him now, that hawk-faced woman with the black teeth. And she seemed immediately imperiled. He had an impulse to shout a warning.

No doubt it was silly to feel this way, thousands of miles removed from the court—to take seriously the ravings of an obscure fanatic whose very face he had not seen. Yet the sight of that tense rigid back, and the sound of that voice among the shadows, alarmed Talbot.

Ratface whispered, "Come, *señor*. The draft will blow out the candles."

He closed the door gently, almost reverently.

"He will remain on his knees like that all this night through. Ah, a great and pious man, my master!"

It had been in Talbot's mind to feign further inebriation and throw himself upon the floor of the common sleeping room. But for a very human reason he changed his mind. He had been unsettled by the sight of the illustrious Don Ernesto and he really felt a need for wine. So he went downstairs again, with Ratface prattling at his side.

As soon as he sat down he wished that he hadn't. For he recognized a man at the next table, who, worse, might have recognized *him*.

Talbot would hardly be watchful for familiar faces in this hot little town on the fringe of civilization; yet he knew instantly that he had seen this man before, though it was some time before he could remember the occasion.

A thin dry face, with a little thin white scar at the chin.

Finally it came back to him.

Standing at the rail of the *Pascha*, watching Don Alvarez de Ruidiaz being rowed back to his own vessel for resumption of his voyage to Spain with cochineal, pearls, cinnamon, and magic water—*there* he had seen the face! It was the face of one of the four seamen in that boat, one of the oarsmen. Talbot had stared at the fellow deliberately, and the fellow had stared at him. Had the man recognized him now? And why, if Don Alvarez had broken his word and turned back, why was not Nombre de Dios in arms on the beach side?

The only explanation Talbot could find was that Don Alvarez had hailed a westbound ship soon after he sailed away from the *Pascha* and had transferred to it a seaman who either was seriously ill or badly injured or else who was showing symptoms of a serious contagious disease.

That could be it.

Again Talbot glanced at the man, who was gazing at him. The man wore a puzzled frown. He was trying to remember where he had seen Talbot's face.

Talbot rose, simulating drunkenness with such emphasis that even his chattering companion became aware of it. Talbot slapped the little fellow across the shoulders, and staggered for the stairs.

In the common room he divested himself of armor, doublet and shirt. He resumed the doublet and steel and tucked the shirt under the breast plate, from whence he could tug it quickly. This was for identification purposes. Each of Drake's men when they landed would be wearing a white shirt tied around his left arm, so that they wouldn't shoot at one another.

He stretched out on the floor about halfway between the window and the door. Had he not been so tired he would not have aspired to sleep in that harness and without as much as a blanket beneath him; but as it was, he had barely felt the boards when he fell off.

The next thing he knew there was a terrible light in his eyes, stabbing them. He did not pop those eyes open, only slitted them to peer.

Actually the light came from a single candle, but the candle was in the hand of the oarsman of Don Alvarez's cockboat, who was leaning low over Talbot.

"Um-m-m," said the oarsman thoughtfully. Talbot did not like the way he said it.

After a while the man went away.

Groggy though he was, Talbot sat up. He heard no bells and so could not know how long he hed slept. The window told him little; there were stars, but there was no moon. The two drunks in the room with him snored on, but no new ones had come. The clatter of talk downstairs might have been a little less loud, and certainly the street sounds were fewer.

Every muscle of his body pleaded with him to lie down again, to fall back asleep. But he shook his head, forcing himself to think.

A bell tolled, up on the Plaza, where, he remembered now, there was a church.

Midnight.

If he did fall asleep again he might well sleep right through the time of the landing, and be lost to his comrades—and quite possibly left here in Nombre de Dios. That is, if he wasn't taken first by the soldiers summoned by that oarsman.

He could think of only two other places to go, to hide. If he could get out of this house quietly enough, having paid for his wine, and avoiding the oarsman, he might unobtrusively make his way to the beach, where at this hour it was not likely that anybody would be loitering. There he might sleep on the sand near the customhouse, and the landing party just before dawn would itself wake him.

On the other hand, if he was being sought as one of El Draque's men, a spy, he must certainly avoid the beach. He must not lead them there.

The alternative, as he saw it, sitting in that dim room, holding his head, was the *maison de tolérance* in the—where was it?—he had marked the name—ah, yes! the Calle de Nuestra Señora de la Purisima Concepcion! He had not looked into that establishment. It had no sign, no red light; nor did any of the inmates show themselves at the window, the curtains of which were carefully drawn; and indeed, Talbot had not seen a single woman of any sort since he entered Nombre de Dios, and he could only suppose that the colonists kept them indoors, after the Spanish fashion in Europe, a heritage from the Moors. All the same, he was sure of the nature of that building and of the trade that went on there.

It was midnight now, a little after. Perhaps the rush hour had passed, and if he deemed it inadvisable to try the beach he might be welcome in the Calle de Nuestra Señora de la Purisima Concepcion for a few hours? They wouldn't ask questions in a place like that. They were not interested in accents, only in cash. And the curtains of course would remain pulled.

It was worth remembering, anyway.

With a great effort, aching, he rose. He retrussed himself, tightened his sword-belt, and put on his morion, tilting it low over his eyes.

When he opened the hall door the sound of Don Ernesto's unending prayer swirled in. He frowned, at the same time shivering. The danger that threatened Talbot downstairs, outside, was a material comprehensible thing which he could meet, he hoped, like a man. But what could anybody do against the congregated might of such fanaticism as that of Don Ernesto Jesus de Santillana y Canovia? *That* was something courage and wit and rapier play could not combat.

Talbot moved to the head of the stairs.

The praying never ceased. It was sibilant now, susurrant. It irritated him, but frightened him too. He was trying to ignore it, lest it unnerve him. For a more immediate peril faced him.

He crouched low, peering through the railing. Don Alvarez's seaman was near the street door, talking earnestly to a couple of soldiers. The soldiers nodded, dubious but interested. All three started toward the stairs.

A more immediate peril, yes. And the best way to meet it, he thought, was to go toward it. He started downstairs.

He stumbled, purposely. He lurched against the rail. He produced another succesfull hiccough.

The proprietor approached, jabbering something about the price of the last two drinks. With an impatient gesture Talbot started to toss him a coin—but here one of the soldiers interfered.

The soldier pushed the proprietor aside. Somewhat frightened, yet firm, he took Talbot's right arm.

"If the *señor* will accompany us outside for a little walk I think he will find that the night air—"

"To hell with the night air!"

Talbot shoved him away, muttering something about being able to breathe the night air without the aid of any dog of a guardsman. He could read in the fellow's manner that the morion and body armor had impressed him, for all the ragged appearance of the hose and doublet. On the word of a single seaman whose memory had perhaps been befuddled by wine, Talbot believed, they were not likely to arrest one who might after all prove to be a *caballero* of some consequence. They only wished to question him with apparent casualness while he seemed drunk. They could assert, if there were trouble afterward, that they had been trying to help the gentleman.

But had the seaman's story convinced, after all? The soldier on the right was a persistent fellow. He took Talbot's arm again, this time with a firmer grip, while at the same moment the other soldier took Talbot's left arm. And the sailor from the carrack pointed at Talbot, shrieking:

" 'Tis the very same man! I swear it by all the saints!"

They started to push Talbot toward the door.

CHAPTER ELEVEN

The time for mummery had passed. Talbot stepped backward, twisting. His left arm came free; but for all the surprise this movement caused, the persistent soldier clung to the right arm. Talbot hit him full in the mouth.

The man dropped Talbot's arm, putting both hands to his mouth, while his eyes became enormous. Before he could realize what had happened, Talbot had struck him again. The man stumbled back into a chair. *"Dios!"* he muttered. Then he sprang to his feet, drawing.

They all drew.

Talbot had jumped half across the room, but though he was able to reach the door he did not dare to pause at the latch. He wheeled, sheathing his dagger, meeting the attack of the two soldiers with rapier alone. He thought he could hold them off for a few moments. He made no attempt to cut or thrust, but only parried with a wide flashing counter. Meanwhile his left hand fumbled with the latch behind him.

Somebody threw a stool, which struck him on the left leg. Then the door came open, and Talbot unhesitatingly sprang backward into the street. He didn't linger to make any gallant gesture. He ran.

Up one street, down another. They were narrow thoroughfares but straight, unlike those of Europe; and they were mercifully dark tonight.

There were shouts behind him, the sound of running feet, and somebody discharged a musket.

Windows were being opened, curtains drawn, and men were calling questions.

Talbot had stored in his memory a good idea of the city's streets, but soon, in spite of this, he was lost. He only knew to lead the chase generally up the slope away from the beach, the customhouse.

He rounded a dim corner, ran full-tilt into four or five men with drawn swords. He lowered his head and dashed through. He was past them before they were able to turn in their tracks.

He burst into the Plaza, the center, the hub of Nombre de Dios. Before him loomed the Governor's house, ghostly yellow in the starlight. Now, again, he knew where he was. He ran around the Governor's house to the south; and a moment later he was tipsily knocking at the house in the Calle de Nuestra Señora de la Purisima Concepcion.

They were in no hurry to open—he had already tried in vain to open the door himself—and he chafed, since at any moment this street might be thronged with soldiers.

But when the door was, at last, opened, he forgot about soldiers.

He had expected a bully, a pimp, or else a painted, simpering, four-chinned procuress. But the woman who stood there was tall and shapely. She carried a lighted candle, and was wrapped from chin to toe in a loose plum-colored silk robe. Her hair, raven-black, was piled high on her head and caught there with silver combs. She

94

was pale, and had a slow sleepy smile, and watchful, slitted, dark-hazel eyes.

"You come late, *señor.*"

Talbot made a leg, his hand over his heart.

"But avidly, *señorita,*" he said.

Bowing before a trollop was hardly recommended practice for one who like Talbot was a fugitive. But he didn't overdo it. Though she had made no move to invite him, and indeed stood in the middle of the doorway, he pushed past her and entered the house.

She turned, carelessly closing the door. Her eyes were shrewd.

"The *señor* is precipitous," she murmured.

"The *señor,*" the *señor* said, "has been at sea for a long time."

She smiled, a shade crookedly, always watching him. With her free hand, behind her, she slid the bolt into place.

"I perceive," she murmured. "Ah, forgive me! How clumsy!"

To close the door she had taken her left hand from the upper folds of her robe, and that robe fell open, exposing her.

"I am so sorry!" she cried, and quickly drew the robe together again.

She was stark naked underneath. Talbot Slanning had seen, if briefly, a magnificent bare body. He shuddered, catching up his breath. His eyeballs throbbed. His mouth went dry.

It was of course an old trick of the trade. Not for an instant did Talbot suppose that it had been a slip. His common sense told him to discount it and to pay attention only to his real business, which was that of lying low for a little while. But common sense can be limited under these conditions.

95

He almost grabbed her. It might be better to see that body again, stare at it, since he was about to pay for its use; it could be settling to gloat over it. Yet he succeeded, somehow, in seeming flippant. He smiled acknowledgment and admiration.

"Perhaps a jack of wine first?" he muttered. "So that we will become better acquainted?"

This might have puzzled her, but she smiled.

"It the *señor* will come this way ..."

She crossed the small entrance hall and opened a door. There was a light, a mere candle stub, in this room. There was also a bed. The bed was large, and it looked clean. It looked cool.

He followed her, and turned to her. She did not let the robe fall open again, she was too intelligent for that. She laid a hand on his bright breast plate,

"It seems so harsh ... it is hard to think that a heart beats under here."

"It is not the heart that we are thinking of, my dear," Talbot said. "Now, fetch the wine."

She actually did blush. She nodded her head, always looking at him.

"Yes, I'll get the wine," she whispered, and then she was gone.

She closed the door behind her. There was no latch on the outside. He had noted this.

He strolled about, though there was not much room. His cue was to get undressed—surely he would not be prepared for pleasure whilst he wore armor and a long sword. However, he could not forget an old adage, one of the soundest: *Never trust a whore.*

Had she given out giggles, or had she been sullen and slatternly, he would have stripped without hesitation.

Instead, he went to the window.

It was small, but not too small to get through. There

was no glass in it, only a shade that had been raised. This was the back of the house, and the window faced out upon a small courtyard, from which, on the far side, an alley ran into shadows—presumably to the next street. The courtyard was bare. Nor were there any lights.

Here was a bad moment for Talbot Slanning, seared by desire; and as a more religious man might have reached by instinct for a rosary or the Bible, he drew his sword.

Somehow the grip of his sword might restore his senses.

He made a few idle passes. There was not much room.

He sheathed when he heard or thought he heard a sound in the entrance hall. He did not open the door to that hall, but he went to it and put his ear against it. Was that whispering? He could not be sure.

Never trust a whore!

He went back to the window. Had that bitch sensed that he was a wanted man and that she might get more money by summoning the watch than ever she could get by writhing on the bed with him?

He had shown no coins and never even mentioned them, nor had she mentioned them, in itself a suspicious circumstance.

The courtyard remained bare and utterly silent. It was odd how much silence could be crammed into this small space, when elsewhere in Nombre de Dios many men frantically sought him.

What was that? It could have been the click of a latch just to the right of this window. It *could* have been somebody about to leave this house by a courtyard door—to cut off his escape.

"I—I have brought the wine."

He whirled around.

She was standing there, a few feet from him. She had closed the door. She no longer held a candle, only a jack

97

of wine, and in her eyes there was still that odd faraway smile. She reached out with the wine. She made no pretense of holding the plum-colored robe together at her neck.

The robe, then, fell fully open. She shrugged, and it slithered off her shoulders. It covered no more than her left arm as she held the wine toward him.

The candle fluttered.

"Lady," he whispered, "I think you're too late."

He jumped out the window.

A shadow loomed at his side, and somebody grunted. Talbot was snicking out his dagger, but he did not pause for a scuffle. He ran out the alleyway.

He collided with somebody. He couldn't see a thing. He slashed wildly, and ducked, and ran on.

It was not a blind, thank God. He came upon a street. At the loft, men were running toward him, and he could catch the twinkle of steel. He turned right.

Now he knew that he could not really escape. However fleet he might be, howsoever agile at dodging and twisting and doubling, inevitably they would run him to earth. For there were guarded walls on three sides of him and water on the fourth, and within this narrow compass, even the most inefficient searching force soon would be able to ferret out a fugitive.

There was no place where he could hide for more than a few minutes. There was no place, as he knew from his afternoon's inspection, where he could hope to scale the wall without being seen.

And it was at least two hours before Francis Drake would come.

As before, he had led the chase away from the beach. Very soon he found himself gazing across a garbage-strewn market place at the inside of the Panama Trail gate.

A soldier in the watchtower, having heard the sounds of chase, was leaning over the parapet calling questions. Another soldier, below, was whirling a torch around and around, striving to bring it to full blaze. Gray figures were tumbling out of the long barracks building. Somebody discharged a musket. Back in the Plaza a brazen alarm bell was being rung.

Would it be wisest to surrender? He might convince the authorities that all the hubbub had been no more than a drunken brawl. Or, if they did not believe this, what else could they get from him inside of two hours? He had never been tortured, but he thought he might hold out for two hours anyway. Their most exquisite questioning would take time, time being of the very essence of torture. And a violent, hurried examination of Talbot might kill him before he could blurt Francis Drake's secret.

After all, it was his word against that of a sick seaman. And surely he could continue for some time his pretense at drunkenness; surely he could concoct some story that they would find it impossible to refute within two hours.

There was no way to warn off Captain Drake. The best that Talbot could hope to do was lull local suspicions, if only for a little while.

Yes, he would surrender.

He drew a deep breath. He staggered out of an alley and into the discouraged starlight of the market place. His chin was low, and he blubbered to himself, reeling.

An under-officer accosted him. What was the trouble? What was all that noise back there?

This fool would not suppose a lone drunkard to be the cause of all the stir. He would have pushed impatiently past Talbot. But now Talbot wished to be arrested as ardently as a few minutes earlier he had wished to avoid arrest. He stumbled against the under-officer, bumping him.

He was shoved away and cursed.

"*Mierda!*"

Snarling, Talbot struck the officer on the nose.

A rapier flashed.

"Drunken dog! I'll teach thee to—"

The under-officer never quite knew what happened after that. His blade was thrown so high that he barely kept his grip on it, and his right shoulder was bitten twice by what might have been a lick of flame. He stepped back, sobbing.

But Talbot, instead of pushing to an easy victory, spun on his heel and raced back into the shadows of the alley. For at the instant the under-officer drew, Talbot had heard from the direction of the customhouse a shrill high whistle, followed by a splatter of musketry, and then—delightful sound! heavenly sound!—the well-remembered bellow of Captain Francis Drake, carrying even over the babble of the town, carrying clear here, to the Panama Trail gate.

"*Hal-lo, Slanning! Ahoy, Slanning! Ahoy!*"

CHAPTER TWELVE

Now nobody moved to stop him. For a split second he had the world to himself. Doubtlessly such pursuers who had any clear idea of whom they were pursuing had been thrown into bewilderment by the shouts in a foreign tongue issuing from another part of the town.

Most of the residents appeared to be suffering from the belief that Nombre de Dios was being assailed by the Maroons, and the clamor and confusion were frightful.

Talbot ran, laughing. He laughed at the thought that twice within an hour he had fled from sword fights. Those were the first two times in his life. Would they be the last? Assuredly the court ruffler had cooled.

He avoided the Plaza, for he could see that most of the population instinctively was making for that center. Alleys and side streets led him at last to the slope that ended in Francis Drake.

The Captain was crisp, curt, loud. He anticipated Talbot's question.

"We were early, and they were twitchy, so I declared that it was already dawn—and we came in. The battery?"

Talbot yelled: "Only two sentries, and they'll run. Six

brass pieces, eighteen-pounders and eleven-pounders. But they can't be fired tonight."

"Good. Put the shirt around your arm or you might be killed."

Men were scrambling out of cockboats, jumping to the dock, or else wading, splashing, while they held their weapons high. They were worried men, unsure of themselves.

"John! Oxenham! Gillard! Along the beach to the watergate, and smash it. Then the Plaza. We rendezvous there. Hurry. And—make noise!"

Some of the men carried pikes and some carried fire-pikes; a considerable number had long bows; there were a few with partisans; but there were some muskets as well.

A drummer and a trumpeter ran off with the party dispatched along the beach, making the noise of half a regiment. Another drummer and another trumpeter stayed with Captain Drake.

Hixom had been told off, with six men, to guard the pinnace and the cockboats.

The rest started up the slope toward the Plaza, Captain Drake leading them, Talbot at his side. The Captain was gay in scarlet silk, a silver whistle swinging on a cord around his neck. He had his rapier in one fist, a dagger in the other, and he shouted without pause. Indeed, they all shouted. That was orders.

Talbot screamed into the Captain's ear: "The Governor's house is weaker, in the Plaza!" The Captain nodded, without ever having ceased to shout.

Nobody approached them or hailed them on the way up the slope, but the Plaza itself was bright in the red glare of torches, and several hundred men were drawn up before the Governor's house. The two front ranks consisted of soldiers, most of them with muskets raised.

It was amazing that the Spanish soldiers had been so fast.

Somebody shouted *"Fuego!"* and then it was as though the whole square had exploded.

The trumpeter whirled twice, started to run back toward the water front, and fell on his face. Two men dropped to their knees—though whether from wounds or simply from fright it was not possible, then, to know. Talbot felt the morion pushed down upon his forehead as though somebody had struck him with a club, but he was more immediately aware that Francis Drake had lurched against him. He grabbed the Captain.

"You're hit!"

"Sh-sh! The men are panicky enough now."

The Captain raised his voice to a shout again, and he charged across the square, brandishing his rapier. He limped the least bit on his right leg, but only Talbot, looking for it, noticed this. Talbot, close behind him, yelled for him to keep his point in line.

"How d'ye hope to parry when—"

"I'm not parrying tonight—I'm cutting!"

It seemed to Talbot for a moment that only he and Drake had charged. They were surrounded, and his own sword was kept so busy that he had no chance to scold the Captain again. He ran one man through, chased away two others. Something smashed against his back and bore him to the pavement, but he sprang to his feet again, slashing.

There was so much noise around him that there seemed to be no noise at all. There in the wild red torchlight he had the conviction that he was fighting in an utter silence, as if in a nightmare, in a fog of stillness, fighting phantoms with a phantom blade.

And then, abruptly, he wasn't fighting at all, but running here and there to carry out the commands of the

103

Captain. From a street at the east end of the Plaza the other half of the invading force had appeared, shouting and singing, with drum and trumpet; and the Spaniards, who in fact outnumbered their foes five to one, but could not be expected to know this, broke and ran.

It was not a rout. They knew where they were running. But for a little while, at least, they left the Plaza to the English.

"The ram! Where's that ram!"

A fourteen-foot tree trunk, into the sides of which iron pins had been driven, was hauled into the Plaza. So swiftly had the fighting there been finished that the men who bore this ram had not been given a chance to catch up with their fellows—until this moment. But they asked no questions; and soon the thing was thunking regularly against the door of the Governor's house—the west door, the one Talbot already had pointed out as the weakest.

John Drake was posting pickets at the head of each street opening upon the Plaza. Talbot, tearing the shirt off his left arm, crowded the Captain into a dark doorway.

"I tell you the men—" Drake protested.

"The men will have no leader at all if this wound's not staunched. Hold still a moment."

It was secretly done, as though it were a shameful deed. The wound was high, near the groin. It was a ragged, a nasty gash; and Talbot, seeing it, wondered how Drake could keep fighting. Talbot bound it with merciless pressure, tugging with all his strength; and afterward he covered much of the white shirt with the Captain's trunk hose, lest the men see it.

The Captain should have screamed; but he was too wildly impatient to feel any pain. His feet shuffled, and

104

his eyes moved back and forth, watching everything in the turbulent square, while Talbot bandaged the leg.

The instant Talbot finished, the Captain shot away like a stone released from some siege machine.

"Take care you don't run too hard!"

The Captain paid no attention; Talbot ran after him.

The men were frightened, looking for a counterattack. The very *absence* of Spaniards was ominous—yet they did not dare to pause while Francis Drake roared at them.

"*Swing* on that ram! *Swing!*"

The door, splintered, shrieked like an animal in pain. The Captain squirmed and wriggled through the aperture. Talbot, snatching a torch, followed.

Talbot shouted: "The cellars!"

In fact there was only one cellar, and it was enormous. There was only one door to it, and Talbot and Francis Drake together were able to batter that down almost before Oxenham, Tom Gillard, and three of Ranse's men came scurrying after them.

Two of Ranse's men carried torches, and these, with the torch Talbot had snatched up, showed them silver.

It was more silver than most of them ever had supposed to exist. It was a mountain made of bars neatly crisscrossed. A mountain? No rather it was like a huge silver house, though it was solid, not hollow. It extended almost the length of the cellar, perhaps seventy-five feet; and it could have been twelve feet wide, ten feet high.

This great wall shone white and luminous, as though there was a strong light behind it. It did not shimmer, even in the jerky glare of the torches, but shone with bland unwinking magnificence, with splendor serene and tranquil.

They stepped back, jerking in their breaths—all excepting the Captain, who went without hesitation to one corner of this house and because the top was too high for him to reach started to strike a corner with the heels of his hands. He dislodged a bar, causing a landslide of silver: he sprang back barely in time to prevent his feet from being crushed.

Calmly he picked up one bar. Contemptuously he surveyed it.

"Silver," he muttered, as though to himself. "Thirty-five or forty pounds. No. We're for elsewhere. Come on."

"I'll summon the men," said Gillard."

"Wait!"

Gillard paused.

"This is not what we came for," the Captain said. "We came for gold, not silver. Leave it. We'll smash the Cabildo."

"My regrets," Talbot murmured. "It was something I couldn't learn."

"Not your fault, Slanning. Come along."

"By God, man, have you gone mad?" Gillard cried.

The Captain's eyes were icy, his mouth was tight.

"Nay, I'm sane enough, Master Gillard. There's maybe three hundred and fifty tons of metal here. Even if we could hold the town long enough to cart it to the boats, 'twould sink them. We'll take none. We came for gold."

"Angels of grace! A million pounds sterling, and you'd walk away from it as if it was a pile of horse manure!"

"As far as I'm concerned, Master Gillard, it is. No, I'll not walk away from it—I'll *run* away. Come on."

The Cabildo was not far away. The battering-ram could be used again. Already orders against looting had been issued, but now Captain Drake made specially sure that none of the men would enter the Governor's house and see that silver.

Afterward he ran down to the Cabildo, with Talbot at his heels anxiously watching him, marveling that the man could still stand.

106

"*Here* we'll find gold!"

But even as the ram started its work—much harder here, for the street was narrow and slanted, so that the men on one side were lower than those on the other— the door was much stronger too—the Captain leaned against a pillar, gasping.

Talbot took his elbow.

"You'll faint?"

The Captain's face gleamed with sweat, but somehow he shook his head.

"I never faint," he whispered arrogantly.

The real dawn was coming—not the false one the commander had hailed—and the sky was a sickish gray. Nombre de Dios was filled with little groups of men hurrying here and there, peering around corners, creeping with caution from doorway to doorway. Now and then a musket would be discharged, and there would be some yells, and scampering of feet. Then silence again—except for the monotonous thunking of the ram, which resounded through the whole town.

What were the Spaniards doing?

The Spanish soldiers hadn't been sure of themselves, sure of the odds they faced, they soon would be. Daylight would help them. Daylight would be fatal to the English.

"Slanning, go to the Plaza and tell my brother to defend that place at all costs. Then seek out Tom Gillard and tell him to march his men down to the customhouse and make sure that all's well with the boats. When we go we must go very fast."

"Are you all right, sir?"

"I'm all right. I'll keep leaning against this post, and the men won't see. Tell Gillard to report to me here, afterward."

The rain came without warning. It was not drops but

sheets. It hurled itself upon the housetops, the streets, every exposed thing, fuming, stingling, hissing a song of hate. And thunder boomed and crashed.

Talbot, making sure that Tom Moone was aware of his master's condition and that he would keep this information from the others, dashed for the Plaza.

He was an aide, a courier, with no command of his own. It was normal that he should be given such an assignment.

The houses of Nombre de Dios, and in particular the buildings fronting upon the street up which Talbot ran, like those of the Plaza itself, offered some shelter from the rain. There were wide verandas, deep doorways, many arcades. Talbot ignored these. He kept to the middle of the street. The rain threw itself against him as though in an effort to knock him down; it splattered and splashed off his morion, and seeped through the cloth of his sleeves and of his hose, and it slithered under the back and breast plates, a stealthy menace. The street itself, dry a few short minutes before, had become a raging torrent. Brown water swished and splashed in a thousand streams on its way toward the beach. Great brown pools lay shuddering under the impact of the rain, their surfaces a frothy blur. Rain was lashed and whipped against the sides of houses, splitting into billions of tiny iridescent drops, into a haze that was almost a fog.

Forty men, more than half the force, had been delegated to guard the Plaza, but only a few of these were in sight when Talbot crested the slope. The others were standing under cover keeping their weapons dry. John Drake and a few others tramped back and forth, closely watching the streets that led to the back of the town. John Drake roared continuously; but whether he did this in sheer exuberance or whether he was trying to sing, nobody knew.

"Aye, we'll hold it—if we're not drowned first!"

"You should see it below," Talbot told him. "Where's Gillard?"

"Gone with four men out to the east wall, to make sure there's no flanking. All in high chafe too, for that he's obliged to take orders from me. I don't like that man, Slanning."

Talbot grinned.

"Neither do I," he said.

"He stamped about like Tom-o'-Bedlam when first he came from the Governor's house. Tell me, what did ye find in there, Slanning? Frank was too busy to give me that information."

"Silver."

"Oh? Much silver?"

"About three hundred and sixty tons of it."

"I see."

"Tom Gillard was all for toting some away, but the Captain, your brother, swore that 'twas not worth the effort to go staggering off under such cheap metal."

John Drake dashed his helmet to the mud and threw his head back, roaring with delight while the rain water streamed down his face.

"Oh, Frank! Frank!"

"He said he'd come for gold and gold he would get!"

"And he will too, Slanning! Mark my word, he will! I know him! He'll be the richest man in England—or else the deadest one in America!"

Talbot left him and made along the street leading to the east wall.

It was past the proper hour for dawn, but the sun was hidden behind thunderclouds and unceasing rain kept the town in darkness. Near the east wall Talbot saw ahead of him a group of four or five men who crouched in the shelter of a porch. He jumped behind an arcade

109

pillar. These could have been Gillard's men, or they could be Spaniards edging their way around to the Plaza as scouts in advance of a larger force. To Talbot they were but vague forms, darker blurs in the dark street. He hoped for a flash of lightning,but none came. It was a shout from the group that reassured him. They had seen him, and they were English.

"Hi! What make ye there?"

It was Tom Gillard's voice. Talbot without hesitation stepped from behind the pillar.

"Orders from Captain Drake that—"

There was a flare of orange-colored light, and an explosion. Something clanged against Talbot's breast plate with such force that he was pushed over backward and sat in the mud with an angry ignominious splash. Startled, he felt with a hand the left side of his breast plate. It had been groved, but not torn: its curved steel had spared him a bullet in the heart.

"Arse holes! Don't you know I come from Captain Drake? Didn't I call out!"

Tom Gillard, who held a smoking pistol in his hand, smiled at him in mock astonishment.

"In this wind, in this rain, who could say that a shout's in English or in Spanish? You might have been a trooper who'd climbed the roofs from a back street."

Talbot rose, and his hand was on the hilt of his rapier.

"The command," Gillard drawled, "was that each of us should wear something white upon his left arm. I see nothing of that nature on yours."

It was true that Talbot's arm was not marked now, for the shirt had been used to bandage Francis Drake's leg. It was also true that Gillard had not mistaken him for a Spaniard. Yet, Gillard was sure of himself, as always. Slaughterous intent could not be proved against

110

him. His expression told Talbot all that Talbot needed to know; but you can't put a man's expression into your purse and produce it later as evidence before an impartial judge; you can't establish a man as a criminal on so slight a thing as the glint in his eyes or a lift at the corners of his mouth.

Talbot's whole battered body, all his muscles and his nerves, implored him to draw and to have at this taunting giant. His temples throbbed; his hands twitched; there was a weird moaning in his head.

Tom Gillard continued to smile. It was a smile that challenged Talbot to draw. Gillard would have liked nothing better.

Talbot caught his breath in full, and held it like a diver. He exhaled suddenly, noisily, and then inhaled again. He took his hand from the sword-hilt.

In a low harsh voice he gave the Captain's orders. Gillard actually bowed.

"We will do as the Captain says, of course," mocked Gillard. "Ho, boys! Follow me."

Abruptly the thunderstorm ceased. Everything was abrupt in this country! As though at a signal no rain fell, where a moment earlier there had been torrents; and a vexed sun, annoyed by the delay, started to shove columns of light down upon Nombre de Dios.

Light, day, meant the end of the attack.

Talbot started slowly back for the Plaza. The thing was lost. It had been hard, and it had failed. Well . . .

He heard the whistle that had been hung around the neck of Francis Drake. *One-two-three! One-two-three!* That would be Tom Moone blowing that, never Francis Drake. For it meant that Drake had fainted—or died. *One-two-three!* It was the signal to retreat.

They hauled the Captain aboard in a sort of hammock

111

rigged for the occasion. He was not dead, but neither was he conscious.

They had almost as much trouble with Talbot Slanning. *He* was sound asleep.

CHAPTER THIRTEEN

Tom Gillard had finished his report.

"And if there's naught else you wish me for I'll go out on deck and see young Master Butterwalk, who has been looking like a new-made widow these days. Perhaps I can cheer his gloomy soul."

Francis Drake was short.

"There's naught else."

Then Talbot reported. All this was for the benefit of a glowering Ranse, who no longer made any pretense of good-fellowship.

Talbot said nothing about his dented breast plate. It would be impossible to prove an attempt at murder, and he did not care to give Tom Gillard the satisfaction of winning an acquittal.

"One thing further," the Captain said. "In your opinion, Master Slanning—for you were there, you saw the stuff —in your opinion, how much of it could we have moved?"

Talbot shrugged.

"Perhaps a ton, even two tons."

"*Two tons!*"

Captain Ranse could contain himself no longer. They were alone in the cabin now, and Ranse stalked back and forth, waving his arms, working his thick black eyebrows up and down.

"Two tons of pure silver, worth four or five thousand pounds of the Queen's money, and ye treat it like dirt!"

Captain Drake, in his bunk, essayed a shrug.

"You would snatch a few thousand pounds and be happy, Captain. But I came here for millions. And I," he reminded, "am commander of this expedition."

"No longer! Our articles of partnership covered and included this one adventure only."

"True."

"And we are not partners now. I've had overmuch of this big talk. I sail for England today."

"I regret to hear that," Francis Drake lied.

"At least I have the shallop and a caravel and my share of the wine."

They had seized a vessel laden with wine in the harbor at Nombre de Dios. With the corpse of the trumpeter, numerous wounds, a few bad memories, and many bitter feelings, it comprised their only loot.

"And you? You remain here?"

"Aye."

"How long?"

"Until I get what I came for."

"You're a fool, Drake. *I* go back to England."

"God be with you," said the Captain.

Glowering, Ranse went out, and as the door was slammed shut behind him, Captain Drake glanced at Talbot.

"Did I not say he was a vulture?"

"He'll tell some cock-and-bull story at home and spread it abroad that it was all your fault."

"No doubt. I expect them to be calling us pirates when we return."

"I wonder what Gillard will do?"

"Spread lies about you and Butterwalk, as Ranse will spread them about me. But soon you will have the same answer. Men who show one thousand percent profit on an investment are not murderers, any more than they are pirates. Gillard has relatives and some wealth of his own. Ranse will put him down on the Continent, or mayhap he'll brazen it out by asserting that the news of Monckton's death had not reached the Wight when he sailed. With the right connections, even Gillard could buy his way free—though it'd ruin him. For there's always dirty work to be done in Ireland for which the Queen's Majesty has no burning desire to pay in cash. Gillard will turn patriot, forsooth. But you'll not be obliged to behave in that manner, Slanning. Nor will Master Butterwalk."

"Poor Robin! I fear his conscience will rack him always. There was a time when I was affrighted that he'd lose his reason, though I think he's been looking up a bit of late."

"Aye, we'll pump cheer back into him somehow. For there'll be your word and Master Butterwalk's against the word of Gillard as to what happened in that room in the Three Crowns. I'll work as hard for him as for you, Slanning, when we get back."

The Captain, whose face remained bright red for all the blood he had lost, turned his head away and affected a great interest in the ceiling.

"But if the plate fleet's gone—"

"There is a new plate fleet every six months," Francis Drake reminded him. "We missed one. We'll take the next."

"We remain here, then?"

"Aye. We'll cruise a few months, picking up whatever prizes we can—there should be plenty between Cartegena and Nombre de Dios—and then one fine day we'll disappear into Port Pheasant or some such place, and the Spaniards will suppose we've made for home, satisfied with small pickings, even as Ranse is making for home this very day. We'll stock up well, and we'll not venture out until the next treasure has been brought up from Peruana. We'll not attack Nombre de Dios again, for that town will be better garrisoned and fortified now. Panama, at the other end of the bottleneck, is too strong for the force we have. But it should be possible to fall upon the *recuas* as they emerge from Panama."

"Cross the Isthmus?"

"Why not?"

Talbot was laughing, thrilled at the audacious simplicity of this plan.

"For they will not expect us at Panama," Francis Drake pointed out.

"Oh, assuredly they won't!"

"Also, 'twill give us a sight of that great Southern Sea of which we have heard. No Englishman ever has looked upon that ocean, Slanning. And methinks—"

A shot rang out. It seemed to shake the whole ship, for this was the hour of the siesta, and the *Pascha*, at anchor off the Islas de Pinos, had been wrapped in a warm hush.

The Captain whispered: "Close by here! And aboard!"

He could not move, because of his wound.

Talbot ran out on deck. Captain Ranse was at the rail, about to step down the ladder that would take him to a cockboat. Tom Gillard stood near the after cabins, with one of the *Pascha*'s seamen right behind him.

"Inside, somewhere," Gillard called.

Two cabins opened upon the waist. Between their doors a narrow passageway led into the after superstructure, and there were four additional cabins there, two on each side. Talbot pushed past Gillard and ran into the corridor. He shook the seaman, Dick Turner.

116

"Where did that shot come from? What cabin?"

Dick Turner's face was white and his hand trembled as he pointed to the cabin Talbot himself shared with Robert Butterwalk.

Sharp stinging smoke swam out when Talbot opened the door.

"Robin!"

But Robert was dead. The whole right side of his head was black with powder, and there was a round blue-black hole in the temple. In his right hand, smoke curling from its muzzle, was the same pistol that had caused the death of Sir Francis Monckton.

They roamed the seas, taking such prizes as came easily. At Cartegena they captured a couple of frigates, landed, drove off a company of musketeers, and returned in modest triumph to their own vessels. The men, this time, stood up well under fire. The Captain had been confident that they would.

"Men must be *taught* how to fight," he told Talbot.

They established a base at Port Pheasant and stayed there a fortnight, cleaning the ships, shooting at archery butts, pitching quoits. It was a little paradise, and so too were the headquarters they established soon afterward near the mouth of a river they named after Diego, one of the Maroons.

An oversupply of vessels was their only worry. They did not have enough sailors to man them. The *Swan* they scuttled, and later the *Pascha*, and they burned several smaller ones.

Talbot told Francis Drake about the vow taken by Don Ernesto Jesus de Santillana y Canovia, but the Captain did not seem alarmed.

"I make no doubt many a don has sworn the same."

"If you'd ever seen this man—"

117

"You yourself saw only his back. Can you estimate a man's capacity for being dangerous by the straightness of his spine, eh?"

"If you'd seen him you'd understand," Talbot said.

He did not mention this matter again.

The Captain was walking his own poop within a week of the action at Nombre de Dios, and within another week he did not even show a limp, and was suggesting to Talbot that they resume rapier practice. He was as spirited as ever, and as solemn, as stolid, as sternly just.

His brothers did not fare so well. John Drake was urged into an unwise attack upon a Spanish coasting vessel while Frances Drake was cruising the Main in search of provision ships—and had most of his intestines blown away. He died within the hour. Joseph Drake was one of the first victims of a plague that descended upon their hitherto idyllic establishment on the Rio Diego. That plague cut into their force with a far more telling effect than ever the Spaniards had done. Men turned black, shrieking in delirium, and died.

They raided Tolon, and they took a few more ships with provisions; and at last word was brought from out of the jungle, by Maroons, that the treasure fleet had reached Nombre de Dios from Cartegena.

The Spaniards would be moving the treasure now. There was no time to be lost.

On Shrove Tuesday, February 3, 1573, eighteen white men joined Pedro, the Maroon chief, and thirty of his followers; and for seven days they stumbled and tore through the jungle, up the Cordilleras, until they reached a peak where there was a towering redwood, into the trunk of which steps had been cut. Talbot and the Captain and a few others climbed this tree.

Far away, faintly silver-white, clean and dainty, even

demure, was that body of water that the Spaniards had named the Mar Pacifico or Pacific Ocean. The Englishmen gazed upon it for a long while.

Nobody said a word as they descended. When the Captain did break silence, in camp, it was in a manner characteristic of him. He suggested, commanded rather, that they all kneel in prayer and ask the Creator for strength to live until the day when an English ship would sail that far fabled sea.

"Will you captain that ship?" Talbot asked him, after they'd risen.

"Aye, if the Lord wills it."

"But how to get there? Surely no man could carry even a small pinnace in sections across this Isthmus?"

"The Spaniards build coasting vessels at Panama and Lina, and keep them in that ocean. We could not do that, of course. But there are the straits to the south."

"Only one ship hath sailed through those terrible straits and returned to Christiandom," Talbot reminded him.

"There must some day be a second."

The Captain's voice took on an edge of excitement, unusual in him.

"Think of the riches! Here on the Main there has been some defense preparations, for that the Huguenots have been busy hereabouts, and also myself. But along the coast of this Southern Sea there will be none to expect aught but Spanish ships. Town by town we could take, ship after ship. Why, we could sack a whole continent before ever the news reached Panama!"

Talbot asked quietly: "How could we get back?"

"Aye . . . they'd block the straits against us."

"The world is round."

Drake's head snapped up.

"Are you proposing that we follow in the path of

119

Magellan, eh? Are you proposing that we circumnavigate the globe, without charts, without maps?"

"*He* didn't have any either. And in your own words, sir: 'There must some day be a second time.'"

"Hm-m-m. . . ." said Francis Drake; and he was silent for a long while after that.

Two days later they reached the pampas and no longer enjoyed the shelter of foliage. Three days after that they were within sight of Panama—and incidentally, within sight again of the Southern Sea. They crouched at night in the tall grasses on either side of the trail. They had every reason to believe that the wealth of the New World was to fall into their hands at last. And their hearts beat faster when they heard the faint faraway tinkle of the bells around the necks of mules.

The sound came closer. Not one but many *recuas* were approaching, it would seem. They made this part of the trip, over the pampas, by night, to avoid the killing sun.

Again a small thing brought them defeat. A too-eager sailor sprang to his feet and shouted something, for sheer excitement. A horseman who had been riding ahead of the *racuas* turned promptly and spurred back to the city, firing his fowling piece.

It was savage blacks they feared, not Englishmen; but the effect was the same; the alarm had been given; all hope of surprise, the only way they could win, was gone.

They marched to Veracruz, stormed it, drove out the Spaniards, and held the town for an hour and a half, finding nothing worth a theft. Then, hearing that a relieving force was on the way from Panama, they slipped off into the jungle.

There was nothing to do but return to the Atlantic coast, to their vessels. The trip back was a terrible one. Man after man fell dead by the way. Provisions were low; the trail was rough; the heat maddening. But eventually they did rejoin Ellis Hixom and his rearguard.

Of the seventy-three who had sailed out of Plymouth, thirty-one were left.

Their leader was not discouraged.

"We will remain here for another six months," announced Francis Drake. "There will be another shipment of treasure then."

And truly, half a year later Talbot Slanning found himself once again close to the Panama Trail gate of Nombre de Dios.

He was on the outside of the gate now, standing beside a moss-clogged oak, and concealed about him were thirteen other Englishmen, a few Maroons, and twenty Huguenots under Captain Têtu. A stout fellow, that Têtu, and not one of Ranse's sort. They had fallen in with him at Cattivas, where he was in dire want of water and victuals. He swore that he had been searching for Francis Drake these five weeks past. He was Drake's man. What did Drake wish to do?

Why, Captain Drake had a plan. Captain Drake always did. He believed that the last place in all America where the Spaniards would expect an attack was the south gate, the Panama Trail gate, of Nombre de Dois. For that town, since the original attack of a year ago, had been heavily fortified. Captain Drake, however, proposed to halt a few *recuas* at its back door, and this was why the men waited now, hidden, so close to the walls that all through the night they had heard the hammering of carpenters at work refitting the plate fleet.

Three *recuas* came, careless on this, the last stretch. One had fifty mules, and each of the others had seventy mules. They came all more or less at the same time.

There were guards, oh, of course! But it had been well

arranged, the trap was neatly sprung, and the English seamen nowadays knew how to fight.

"*Nom d'un petit nom,*" whispered Captain Têtu, and he sat down.

It was finished very quickly. Têtu was dying, yes . . . And Dick Turner too, was dying; and sundry Spaniards, too, were either dead or messily close to death; but on the whole, the affair had been easily brought off. And Captain Drake was blowing his whistle: *One-two-three! One-two-three!*

Slowly, for they were heavily laden, they started back for the Rio Francisco. "*Nom d'un petit nom.*" muttered Captain Têtu. "Leave me here to die." It was a pity that they could do nothing else but that. It was a pity, too, that they had to jettison a full fifteen tons of silver, dumping most of this into land-crab holes. But they did save the gold and pearls.

Like pack animals they were, staggering. A sailor came to Talbot and the Captain. "Dick Turner asks for you. He is dying."

"I'll go to him," Captain Drake replied.

"He asks for Master Slanning," the mariner said.

"Eh? Go to him then, Slanning."

Dick had a story not easily told, nor was there much time. It came in gasps. His mother and two sisters lived near Chagford, and he was afraid of Tom Gillard. Gillard could do him much harm. He had been afraid, before this, to tell anybody that he'd seen Gillard coming out of the corridor between the forward cabins only an instant after the sound of the shot that had killed Robert Butterwalk.

"He did it, Master Slanning! I know he did it."

If Talbot had thought fast, then, he would have summoned witnesses.

"He grabbed my jerkin, and he whispered to me that if I ever told what I'd seen—"

But it was not in Talbot to think of witnesses in that instant. All he could think was: *Now it's Robin's fight too —when my sword takes that man, 'tis of Robin I'll think.*

"I was affrighted, Master Slanning. Not for myself but for my mother and sisters. Make no doubt! I saw it in his eyes that he had done it! He went there when Master Butterwalk was enjoying a siesta, and he loaded and primed the pistol, and he murdered him and put the smoking pistol into his hand. I saw it in his eyes."

Robert and Talbot had hunted together; they'd laughed and been boy-fools, confiding preposterous things to one another, and when they grew older they had sat with tall cups of rough Devonshire cider. They'd sat there in the Three Crowns many a time, and spoken of the days when—

The Captain looked up, a shade annoyed.

"If Dick Turner wishes me there—"

"Dick Turner's dead."

The Captain cocked his chin very low, for the load that was on his shoulders. But his eyes went to Talbot.

"If you have any of—"

"I have want of nothing save less chatter!"

"Aye," said Francis Drake; and he walked on in silence. He never knew why his friend Talbot Slanning had spoken in that manner; for Talbot never told—he esteemed it a private matter between himself and one other man.

CHAPTER FOURTEEN

The shaking of the trellis awakened Katherine Abergavenny, and for half a minute she lay confused by sleep, staring at the thing, wondering why it should be agitated on a night of no breeze. Then she realized with a start that the reason must be the presence of somebody below.

She rose, wrapped a cloak around her, went to the window. When she saw the vague formless figure of a man, her first impulse was to scream. This was not an impulse of fear. It was a cool realization that the scream is a woman's best weapon, and in this case might summon servants. Tom Gillard, though for the most part keeping to the seas of late, several times had been seen in the neighborhood of Chagford; and it was possible that he'd won full pardon and was prepared again to wreak vengeance upon such local residents as he believed to be his enemies.

She had opened her mouth—when a long-familiar voice reached her.

"Katherine! My chuck, my sweet, Katherine, come down!"

At first she could not believe it. She stood breathless, her mouth open.

"My sweet! My own sweet Katherine!"

She wheeled. On bare feet she raced through dark halls, down dark steps, and fumbled for and found the side door. An instant later she was pressed against Talbot Slanning, with his arms firm and hard around her.

For a little while they did not speak. They scarcely seemed even to breathe, though their hearts thumped wildly and the blood clamored in their pulses.

"Thou hast been well, my sweeting? Thou hast not been made to suffer because of me?"

She kissed him by way of answer.

"And—no child?"

"No child."

"I called at thy window so that none other should know I'm here. 'Tis but a few minutes at best, my chuck. I must ride hard to be back before dawn."

"It—it's on all tongues that thou'rt with Drake the pirate."

Talbot frowned gently, thoughtfully.

"Drake's no pirate, dear. Or if he be, then I would to God we had a nationful of such pirates. Aye, I have been with him since the time I quit Plymouth fourteen months ago. Didst not hear he's returned?"

"No. I've not been to the village today."

"We came back this morning—yesterday morning by now, eh? And the sheriff's men boarded us as never the Spaniards had dared to do. The decks and cabins were thick with 'em. They have placed the ships and all their cargo in custody, and every man of the ships' companies is under arrest. But Captain Drake himself hath been summoned to the presence of the Queen's Majesty, and he will make it right."

"Thou hast great confidence in this Captain Drake?"

"Aye."

"And thou? Is there not a warrant?"

He smiled, and it was his old smile, the one she loved. Yet this was not the same Talbot Slanning who had said farewell to her at this place fourteen months ago. This man was quieter, darker, grimmer. Here was not a hot-headed young fool, but a man of the world.

"There's a warrant, aye. But—could we not go to some place where it's softer and maybe darker? I could tell you about that warrant afterward."

"Talbot! Not—not in my own room!"

"Why not? It's been a long time, my chuck."

Lazily, later, he said again that there was indeed a warrant for his arrest.

"Both our ships were arrested before I was arrested, you see?"

She did not see, and he looked over at her, smiling fondly.

"No sooner had we dropped anchor when the High Sheriff and his men boarded us with papers. Oh, we were expecting it! We'd learned of it from a fisherman we hailed off Sicily. So the papers were read."

He related that the High Sheriff, with considerable formality, and in a basso fitted to his position, read a paper which ordered to be seized in the name of the Queen's Majesty any and all vessels in which Francis Drake, mariner, of Tavistock and Plymouth, county of Devon, should return at any time from the Spanish Indies or the lands of America, together with all and sundry articles and treasures, whether of gold or silver or precious stones, or any other merchandise whatsoever, which the said vessel or vessels might contain. This document also commanded the arrest of the said Francis Drake, mariner, and of every man who accompanied him and was any part of the company or companies of his

126

ship or any and all of his ships or other vessels. And this until such time as complaints against the said Francis Drake, lodged within this past year by the representatives of His Most Catholic Majesty Philip II, King of Castile, King of Aragon, etc., etc., could be heard and properly disposed of.

"There was a supplemental order commanding the Captain to proceed instantly to Exeter, under guard of course. The court's at Exeter, for that the Queen is on progress. And then the sheriff read the second of his papers."

Talbot smiled a shade wryly when he remembered his feelings as this second writ was read. It was, of course, a special royal warrant commanding the arrest of Master Talbot Slanning, gentleman, erstwhile pensioner to the Earl of Sussex. It would mean the Question.

With a sigh, in the darkness, he reached out and touched her bare hip.

Once, on a lark, and thanks to the influence of his master, Lord Sussex, Talbot had gone to London Tower and viewed that machine in the little room with the low ceiling—the machine the jailors called La Gehenna. He wished afterward that he hadn't.

It was a plain, simple, highly polished table, something of a disappointment at first glance. It was only when he had studied it for a while that Talbot saw how diabolically ingenious it was. It was not chipped. No blood stained it. There were no spikes or sharp edges. Yet when a naked man was stretched there, and his wrists and ankles cunningly fastened to pullies above his head and below his feet, the turning of certain wheels that were not even in sight, being underneath the table, could pull him exquisitely apart. If he was lucky enough to faint, the pressure could be slacked off until he had recovered his feeling. If he was very strong and very cour-

127

ageous, or if he couldn't or wouldn't say what his inter-
rogators wished him to say, he might be made to endure
this agony for many hours on end, day after day. Some
of them, Talbot was told, lasted for weeks. Of course it
crippled them, so that they could never walk again; but
even when the rack in itself didn't kill them—and it seldom did—they were ordinarily hanged afterward anyway.

True, the use of La Gehenna was confined to cases of
high treason. But the killing of a personage like Sir Francis Monckton, or any connection with that killing—for
he had been, after all, at least technically, on the Queen's
business at the time—in English law constituted high
treason.

"Would your worship care to try it?" a playful jailor
had asked.

"Ugh!"

His worship might well be trying it in the near future; and as he lay in the darkness he winced at the
thought. He sighed.

"This is better, here."

"What was that, dear?"

"Captain Drake refused to give me up," Talbot went on.
"He said that I had been placed in custody by the first
order, and that I must be treated as a part of the vessel,
like the rest of 'em, like the gold and pearls and silver.
Nobody could touch those things, and similarly nobody
should touch me. Oh, he's shrewd, the Captain is! The
High Sheriff had read his papers in the wrong order. Had
he read the warrant first, it would have removed me from
the ship's company, in the eyes of the law, and afterward the others could be seized, together with the goods
and the ships themselves, by the instrument of the second order. Do you see?"

"No."

"Well, I'm not sure that I do either. Anyway he read the seizure first. Therefore my person was held in the name of the Queen's Majesty, but it was held aboard the ship, and none could remove it, even with a writ of habeas corpus, unless and until the seizure order was amended or superseded by an instrument signed by the Queen's Highness herself. The warrant for my arrest was no such instrument, Captain Drake contended, for it did not specifically provide for violation of the seizure order previously read."

"Oh. But if thou art still under arrest, and the sheriff's men are aboard the ships ..."

He laughed.

"Didst think that sheriff's men could keep me when my own sweet Katherine was but a few short miles away? Nay, but they never knew I left, and they never will know, for I can get back before the dawn. There's a gunport very low to the water. It's low," Talbot went on to explain, "because the ship is low, being filled with treasure."

"You swam?"

"Aye. It was no great matter. The night was dark, and the distance short. Ashore, one who had helped me to escape from England, for a payment, lent me dry clothes and a fast horse. The same man will help me to return. Then I will remain in floating captivity until Captain Drake makes the matter right at court."

Grave always, she pondered this. She thought that he should not have taken the risk. If he were caught, he'd be thought doubly guilty. And she assured him that in the minds of half England he was guilty already.

She told him of Gillard, whom she had not seen but of whom she sometimes heard. Though most of this was not new to him, and certainly no surprise, he listened closely. Captain Drake had predicted well. Gillard, on his return, had made his peace with the throne by throwing upon Talbot all the blame for the death of Sir Francis Monckton, and by offering the services of himself, his shallop, his men, all his possessions. The offer had been accepted. Today Tom Gillard was a bankrupt—but he was alive. He had recently returned from Ireland, and reports had it that he was planning some desperate move to remake his fortune.

"I know not what it is he schemes, but 'tis whispered that he waits for something. The shallop's at anchor in the Catwater, and he never leaves it by day or by night."

"Maybe he'd wait to determine Captain Drake's success at court? He'll see me freed, Katherine, as he himself was freed."

"But he had many to speak in his favor. Besides, he had gold."

"I too have gold, now. Also I have those in high places who will speak for me. Think not that Francis Drake is unversed in politics or that he went upon this voyage all unprepared! Also, my clearance will be a matter of prestige for him."

"He hath an affection for thee?"

"I doubt that. But he can't *afford* to have me disgraced."

But he was doing Francis Drake no notable service now, he reflected. He had made light of his escape from the ship, belittling it; but he knew only too well the risk he was running in order to have those few minutes at Abergavenny Manor.

By God, it was worth it! He kissed her again, and made himself struggle off the bed and reach for his clothes.

He stood at the open window for a little while, breathing the good Devonshire air. He could smell the honeysuckle that climbed the lattice to Katherine's window; he could smell the roses; and he thought that he would even smell the smaller, humbler flowers, the wild flowers tucked away in forgotten places, the violets and pinks and pimpernel and cowslips. After the rank, dank, steaming air of the Darien jungle, this would pleasure the lungs of any true Englishman. After the brash, stifling perfumes of swampflowers that were rooted in black muck, this was a good odor, a clean one, and welcome.

"If there was need for money," Katherine was saying. "I could raise a mortgage on Abergavenny Manor."

"*You* could?"

"The manor's mine now," she said simply. "Father died three days after you went away. He never did recover from that beating."

Talbot said "Oh!" with no particular expression, and stared out the window in the direction of Gillard's Elm.

The girl read his thought.

"Thou must be careful, Talbot! Talbot, my love! Remember the last time!"

"The last time I was not permitted to finish what I had started," he told her. "But when I meet him again, and it will be soon, believe me, my love—when I meet him again . . ."

131

CHAPTER FIFTEEN

Ned Crocker, he of the wineshop in the Barbican, was a man of many enterprises, all shady. In him, as in a corkscrew, it was natural to be crooked. He was a very big man, slow-moving, phlegmatic, and he did not look like a criminal. It is probable that he did not consider himself to be such, and in one sense he was not, being rather a helper of criminals, an abettor of fugitives, one who kept them in concealment, or passed them along, or provided them with such articles as they themselves could not venture out to buy in the market place. His customers were of many nationalities, of many walks of life, though it was true that most of his tasks appertained in some manner to the sea, as did almost everything else in Plymouth; but each of them was able and willing, even eager, to pay in advance for the services he required. When Talbot Slanning and Robert Butterwalk had appeared in Ned's shop and had candidly told him of their predicament, he showed not the slightest amazement or fear or suspicion, but without pause fixed a price. Similarly when, fourteen months later, a signal knock caused him to open his back door and to find there one of those same two young men, dripping wet but with a purse that clinked musically, Ned Crocker instantly made a contract to do as this young man wished.

However, when Talbot returned to Plymouth this night and sought him out at the end of the little stone quay, there was some show of annoyance in the man's flat face. Ned was used to queer customers, but this one seemed intent upon suicide.

"You're late," he muttered. "They'll be changing the watch soon."

Talbot sprang into the rowboat, laughing quietly.

"Pull well for it then, Master Crocker, and trust to God and what's left of the darkness. 'Twas a good mount, and it waits for you right outside the shop. As for these clothes, I'll see that they are returned as soon as I'm free to be about."

Crocker's boat had muffled tholepins, and he himself had much experience in stealth. They made never a sound as they slid out into the Catwater, moving as far as possible in the shadow of the quays and of the anchored vessels. Few lights were visible, and those dim. A mist hung over the water.

The *Swan* and the *Pascha* had long since been scuttled, and the newcomers in Plymouth harbor were captured Spanish ships built in Habana de Cuba by Pero Menendez himself, mightily armed vessels, having been designed for protection of Spanish commerce. They were not large but they were sturdy and extraordinarily fast. They floated very low in the water now, because of their heavy cargoes.

The larger ship of the two, and the faster, Captain Drake's flagship, was named, oddly enough, *El Draque* —the Dragon—the very name the Spaniards had given to Francis Drake himself.

They were near this ship now. They slipped into the

shadow of a shallop, a low slim vessel. Amidships a man leaned on the rail gazing at a dawn-smeared sky. They passed so close that Talbot could almost have stood up and touched the man's arm. Thus Talbot had a good look at him, though the man himself did not even see the boat below, swathed as it was in the shadow.

That face! But where? When? The man was no mariner, for he was small, pale, thin, and there were no rings in his ears. He had a pinched, mean face, the face of a rat.

Already they were drifting past the shallop, and now Ned Crocker was backing water expertly, without a ripple.

Talbot leaned forward, whispering: "Whose boat is that we just passed?"

"Why, Tom Gillard's."

Crocker was squinting across the low restless mist toward *El Draque.*

"I fear you'll have to swim for it, sir. The after watch is awake, and I'll not be able to get close. Leave your cloak and boots here, and when you swim keep your arms under water. I'll row you to the larboard side, and as you crawl through that port I'll make a splash to draw away attention."

Talbot shook his head. He had remembered, now, the identity of the rat-faced man. And something inside of him became very cold, very stiff. He was seeing a weirdly lighted room in Nombre de Dios, and the thin straight back of Don Ernesto Jesus de Santillana y Canovia, and hearing again that toneless ceaseless prayer.

"What does Gillard do these days, Crocker?"

"Nay, what matters that now? Why then, he stays aboard that shallop of his we just passed. He looks to be waiting for something or somebody, mayhap a pardon from London that will let him put his foot on English soil again—publicly, I mean. But he's close-mouthed about it, I can tell you. He never allows any of his crew to go ashore except those who go to fetch supplies or visitors."

"And—those visitors?"

"Sir, we've so little time left. If you're to board the ship before the change of watch you'll have to—"

Talbot repeated: "Those visitors?"

"Spanish gentlemen. Or Portuguese. I know not which. They've been coming down the Exeter road, and are taken out to Gillard's vessel, and afterward they return by the Exeter road again. They do not tarry in the town."

The Queen was at Exeter!

"And what of supplies? Has he bought much?"

"Aye. The vessel's well stocked."

"But I've heard it that Gillard was penniless."

Crocker shrugged. He had scant patience with these questions. The mist was lifting, the sky growing brighter; and Crocker, already no stranger to the sheriff, did not wish to be discovered in the company of a personage so notorious as Talbot Slanning. Crocker's private opinion was that Master Slanning here was mad; for surely there was no hint of sanity in one who'd escaped from the clutches of an angry monarch only to return there before he was missed?

"He was stripped clean," Crocker answered, "but yet he buys victuals and gunpowder. I know not where he gets it, all this gold he gives."

"Gold?"

"Aye, Spanish pieces. Likely he fetched them from the Americas when he returned with Ranse."

"Tom Gillard," Talbot said slowly, "brought no gold from America."

"Nay, I know naught of that, sir. But if you wish to make ship before the watch changes—"

"Turn back. I'll not swim it. Not now."

135

"Eh? You'd go to France, then?"

For the first time, Crocker reflected, the man was making sense.

"No, not France. I'll return to Tom Gillard's vessel. And without a splash, mind you."

"That's a perilous boat to approach, sir. Gillard don't fancy snoopers."

Talbot shifted close to the oarsman, and dropped a couple of coins into his lap.

"You saw that fellow leaning against the rail, eh? In the waist? I'll take him."

"*Take* him?"

"*Take* him. Carry him off. I've an overpowering desire to speak to that man alone, but it must be in some place where the noise will be of no matter, you understand?"

Crocker believed that he did. Yet—partly in the hope of another coin, but mostly from prudence—he paused.

"Tom Gillard's not a man to be playing pranks with, sir."

"I know that well enough. Here."

A coin was dropped.

"I'll do the taking," Talbot said. "You keep the boat underneath."

Crocker hesitated; for the boldness of the proposal startled even a hardened old sinner like him.

"I'll not put foot on that shallop, sir. They say it's damnation to Hell for any man that does. But if you wish to risk it yourself . . . Well, if aught goes amiss I'll off without a word. And afterward, if they come to me, I'll swear I never so much as saw you before in my whole life."

"That I'd expect, Ned. Fair enough. Now, to that rail. And make never a ripple."

They slipped through water as silent as the morning mist that crawled and writhed low around them. Ratface still leaned on the rail, still gazed at the sky where dawn was washing away the dim discouraged stars. He might have been suffering from sleeplessness or from homesickness. Certainly he did not look like a watch; and this fact troubled Talbot, for the presence of any other man on deck would spoil the sport.

Talbot slipped off his cloak. He had no weapon, not even a dagger, but the cloak would be enough—that and a loop of thin strong twine Ned Crocker had given him.

They were on the larboard side of the shallop, the opposite side from Ratface. Talbot stood on the stern seat and was able to reach the rail posts. He drew himself up without a sound. His cloak was thrown over his left shoulder, and the twine was between his teeth.

He dropped to the deck with no more noise than a cat might have made. He had left his boots in the boat, and there was no metal on him to clang, as there was no leather to squeal.

He looked around, for the first time he was in a position to study the upper-deck pattern of Tom Gillard's vessel. It was conventional enough, if trim. It had about it an air of readiness, efficiency. The skipper, you would say, was an alert man. The deck was no more cluttered than it needs must be. The shrouds were taut, like all the rigging. The courses and tops, like the lateen on the mizzen, were neatly furled, and they smelled clean, as though they had lately been aired. Just below them the bonnets were stored. The spare anchor had been catted and fished, the cable flaked in tiers. As for the deck itself, it had recently been swabbed with vinegar and sand and scraped with metal scrapers, so that it fairly shone. Not a line, not a fall, not a block was out of place.

If there was no light in the binnacle, from which the

137

half-hour glass hung—but no light would be needed now anyway, day having come—certainly everything else had been done that could be done to prepare for a quick sailing. Leather flaps had been fixed into the scupper holes, and there were even pins on the capstan. The gong hung in place beside the jackstaff, a little iron hammer attached to it, so that the helmsman could ring the changes of watch.

But there was no helmsman. There was nobody at all on *Gillard's Pride,* at least in sight, save only the hunched, small Ratface, who leaned on the starboard rail entoiled in dreams.

What was that? Talbot, his joints all jelly, sank into the shadow of the larboard rail. What he had heard, or thought he heard, came from forward, the officers' quarters. But no light showed there, and he heard nothing else. It could not have been Ned Crocker rowing around the stern of *Gillard's Pride* in order to get on the starboard side underneath the leaning figure of Ratface.

Certainly it had not been Ratface himself, for he was as still as any snubbing post.

Crouching, his heart beating harshly, Talbot took another good long look around the shallop.

At last he rose again. He caught in his breath. He unslung the cloak, to hold it before him with both hands, the twine being still between his teeth; and in this way he crept across the deck.

Ratface never heard a thing until the folds of the cloak enveloped him. *Then,* perhaps, he cursed or screamed; but the cloak permitted no sound to escape, and the loop of twine had followed the cloak with lightning speed, fastening Ratface's arms to his sides.

Talbot lifted this bundle—Ratface was a little man, not heavy—and with elaborate care, as though he handled some priceless piece of statuary, he slithered it over the rail to Ned Crocker, who expertly caught it and lowered it to the bottom of the boat.

"Ho! What make you here?"

Talbot wheeled—to find himself facing Tom Gillard.

Out for a sniff of early air, the master was fully dressed—fully armed too.

But Talbot had one advantage this time: Talbot was not astounded.

Gillard caught in his breath. His hand moved for the hilt of his rapier.

Talbot took two swift steps forward and drove his right fist into the pit of Gillard's stomach. He put behind that punch every ounce of strength and weight in his body. And Tom Gillard, big man though he was, emitted one chopped-off wheezy "*oonck!*" and fell.

Talbot vaulted the rail.

"*Row*, man!"

The boat fairly sprang away; and the mist, disturbed in its languid swirling, was thrown into a puzzled baffled turmoil, rocking this way and that.

The bundle at the bottom of the boat was motionless.

"There's burlap beneath the seat," Ned Crocker grunted. "Wrap him so he'll look like a sack of goods."

"He doesn't move. Did you hit him?"

"No harder'n I had to."

The stone quay was only two hundred feet from the shallop, and soon they scraped the side of it.

"I hit him once." Crocker went on, as he rose. "To keep him quiet. I misdoubt that I killed him."

"I hope you didn't," Talbot muttered grimly. "I have need of this man alive."

It had all happened very quickly. They were quitting

the quay, Crocker seemingly not in the least embarrassed by the load he carried on his back, when the first roars from the shallop testified that Tom Gillard had caught his breath.

CHAPTER SIXTEEN

The first thing Francis Drake noticed at Powderham was that most of the truly important men were wearing leg-o'-mutton sleeves rather than bishop sleeves. He was made glad by this, for he had selected leg-o'-mutton sleeves for himself only after much thought and worriment. Waists, he noted, were narrower, ruffs fuller, capes shorter; shoulders were higher, with padded welts; if the colors were not quite so bright as they'd been the last time he visited court, there was a great deal more bombast, padding. Breasts and legs were made shapely by means of buskin; there were more morions, fewer cabassets and burganets.

Only the hose showed a French influence. Men were wearing shorter hose than they wore when Francis Drake had sailed from Plymouth.

With the Spanish fashions in dress he was in accord, and indeed they were singularly convenient for a man who for more than a year had been obliged to fish his wardrobe from captured Spanish vessels. But the deeper Spanish influences here amazed and alarmed him. There were Spaniards every way you looked. They strutted, seemingly very certain of their place. Unofficially in

attendance, on paper still unrecognized, they behaved
as though in fact they were lords of the Council.

Sundry arrangements over which Captain Drake had
no control, and which he could not have anticipated, had
brought about this change of attitude. There were, properly, in upper circles at least, no English clothing fashions. There was always a certain amount of Dutch influence to be noted in the court that clustered around
Elizabeth Tudor. A man with a quick eye and a knowledge of the world, even a man who like Francis Drake
had been far away from the court for more than a year,
on his return could tell at a glance which way, French
or Spanish, the official wind was blowing. Just now, most
emphatically, it was blowing Spanish; though it had
been French when Francis Drake left.

Sundry arrangements over which Captain Drake had
no control, and which he could not have anticipated, had
brought about this change of attitude, truly a reversal.

Fernando Alvarez de Toledo, Duke of Alva, had been
removed as Governor of the Spanish Netherlands, and
English trade with the Low Countries had been resumed.
More important were the St. Bartholomew's massacres
in Paris and the orgy of slaughter that followed them all
over France. Elizabeth, as the Protestant champion, had
no other choice than to frown upon France after that
hideous affair. And frowning upon France meant smiling
upon Spain: England was too weak even to dream of
being the enemy of both these powers. And so it was
that the Spanish gentlemen flirted their tailfeathers at
Powderham this day, and basked in the sun, while
Francis Drake stood obscurely in a corner.

He was not a man likely to remain obscure.

When the whisper came that the Queen approached,
Francis Drake felt no happier. For the whisper included
some account of the hawking on the way. Soon out of

Exeter, it seems, the hounds had raised a large heron, and Elizabeth Tudor herself had unhooded and unjessed Pride-Girl, her own favorite lanner. But of sport there had been none. Pride-Girl, already fed that morning (which was the fault of the falconers), and unjessed downwind (which emphatically was the fault of the Queen herself) had flown low, refusing to sight the heron, refusing even to answer whistles, and had been lost somewhere in the west. It was humiliating. The Queen knew as well as everybody else that she had been inexcusably maladroit. She didn't fancy disobedience in anybody or anything around her, not even a bird. Besides, Pride-Girl had been expensive.

In addition, the whispers had it that the Queen's health was no better. Francis Drake, like dozens of others, wondered as he was pushed back against a wall, unbonneting, how much the future of England might depend upon the state of that unpredictable royal digestion.

Gentlemen came first, in pairs, and then the barons, the earls, the knights of the Garter. The Lord Chancellor waddled across the courtyard, and the Lord Treasurer, the Lord Privy Seal, the other lords and knights of the Council. There were the gentlemen-pensioners, who seemed to go by interminably, each in full armor, each preceeded by a servant who held upright before him a gilded battleaxe. There were the much younger, tougher gentlemen and yeomen of the guard, halberdiers in bright scarlet. There was an official who bore a bunch of bright seals aloft on a red silk cushion, and one who bore before him, point-up, encased in a red scabbard studded with golden fleurs-de-lis, the sword of state; also one who carried the sceptre—not the real sceptre but a cheap duplicate sufficient for minor state purposes such as this—on yet another scarlet silk pillow. There were the maids of honor and the ladies-in-waiting, each her-

143

self attended by one or two maids as well as by a small male page. There was a fanfare of trumpets, a roll of drums. And then there was Elizabeth.

She looked to be in a prodigiously bad humor. She was a thin, rather small woman in gray taffeta, tense, jerky and birdlike in her movements, with a slight limp. The sharp chin was tilted high, and the oblong unsmiling face, washed with pale freckles, was rigid. But the eyes moved. They were small dark peering eyes; and they went back and forth, back and forth, ceaselessly.

If she saw Francis Drake—which was unlikely—she gave no sign. But she was neither smiling nor nodding today anyway. She muttered a few words to Sir William Courtenay, her host; listened expressionless, with automatic patience, to a long Latin ode of welcome recited by an old man dressed, more or less, as an angel; and then swept indoors.

The doors were closed.

The company in the courtyard rose, buzzing.

But Francis Drake was in no mood for gossip. Men were pointing at him, whispering about him. Some, he knew, were calling him pirate. A few were men with whom he wished to talk—but not in this crowded place. Besides, he must speak to the Queen first. Publicly she would no doubt call him names. He didn't care. It was what she said in closet that counted; and it was only in the privacy of the closet that he could promise her, secretly, after his lawyers had finished making their show of papers and ribbons and seals, a juicy portion of the treasure contained in the holds of his two ships. *Then* Elizabeth Tudor would smile, if she dared. It might be that the Spanish pressure would be too strong. He thought that he knew the Queen's personal inclinations (every man in court thought as much, despite innumerable upsets), but he could not predict when or how

144

vehemently she might act upon them, or when she might veer and tack, now sailing straight before the wind, now inexplicably making a great yaw. Spain or France? France or Spain? Which would it be? Who could know?

Drake strolled out of the courtyard and into a small garden at the rear of the castle. It was deserted. At one end a sallyport in the wall was closed but unlocked, and through its bars was visible a footbridge leading across the scummy stinking moat. Captain Drake wondered idly why it was not guarded. There was a horse on the far side of the footbridge: it was a small black horse, and looked fast; the red-leather saddle was high, rather Moorish, and stamped with a device not familiar to Captain Drake—sable, a fess wavy argent, between two inverted axes proper.

These things Francis Drake saw, and fleetingly he wondered at them, as he wondered that so pleasant a place as this garden should be deserted, while men crowded and jostled one another in the courtyard near-by. But mostly his mind was occupied with thoughts of a different nature.

Men erred who supposed that this mariner sought gold only. He was no petty merchant, snatching his gains and hugging them to his bosom. He would alter the trade habits of the whole world. He would singe the beard of the greatest living monarch. A mosquito, he'd bite a lion to death. A mouse, he'd slay an elephant. Of all the treasure that lay in the two vessels in the Cat-water—the treasure for which he had plotted and schemed, and bribed and dickered, and moiled and mucked and fought, for which repeatedly he had risked everything he owned, including his very life and reputation—he did not expect to retain for very long a single coin of that. He thought of it not as a fortune but as a means. He would gladly spend it all, if that were to

145

enable him to go on robbing on the scale of which he dreamed. For he was a true gambler, this thirty-year-old redhead—a gambler who never dragged his winnings across the board, but unfailingly and unhesitatingly permitted them to lie, doubling the stake for the next cast.

His dream now was of that Southern Sea he'd glimpsed, the Pacific. Wrested from Spain, what a field for trade it would make! What an opportunity!

But so much hung now on the Queen. He must fight now not on the half-deck, where he was at home, and happy, but in a world built of whispers, of broken vows, double meanings, cliques, intrigues, unspoken understandings. Neither astrolabe nor good Toledo steel would get him through this maze of personalities; and he was confused, even a mite alarmed.

A menial coughed, bowing.

"Gracious your worship, it is forbidden that anybody be in this garden whilst the Queen's Majesty changes her garb."

"Eh?"

"The Queen's Majesty is with her tiring-women in yonder chamber, your worship."

The menial, without turning his own head that way, indicated two large windows about ten feet from the ground, near the sallyport. The casements were open, but the windows were covered inside by heavy arrases.

"Should it perchance that a breeze stirred the tapestry," the menial explained, "it would be possible for a man in this garden to see that which he should not."

There was something like a grin tugging at the corner of the fellow's mouth.

"For the Queen to retire to an inner chamber, you see, when she wishes to change from her traveling garb—well, it would mean dim light and discomforting warmth."

"Ah," said Captain Drake, and handed the man a

146

cropper. "Thanks for thy warning. I'll quit the place."

He was as near as he ever came to smiling. The Queen's personal modesty was notorious, her virginity something she advertised.

So Francis Drake started hastily after the servant.

He was stopped by collision with the last man on earth he had expected to see.

"*Slunning!* Merciful God, have you gone mad?"

Certainly Talbot Slanning looked the madman. His sword-belt was awry. His doublet and hair —he was without bonnet—were gray with dust. Dust was caked upon his face too, and sifted into the crevices of his features. All this intensified the wild light in his eyes.

He grabbed the Captain's arms, shook him.

"The Queen! Where is she?"

"Safely changing her clothes beyond that arras, so far as I know. Come, come, man, out with it! Babble like this—and somebody will call the guard!"

Talbot tumbled forth the story, gasping for breath. Ratface, whom he had left in the custody of Ned Crocker, had been too badly frightened to do anything but tell the truth.

Don Ernesto Jesus de Santillana y Canovia, back from Darien, had got himself transferred to the household of one of the grandees stationed here as unofficial ambassador in England. He held a petty inconspicuous post. But his vow, and the extent of his fanaticism, were well known to his fellow-countrymen here; and he was being used as an instrument of assassination, a catspaw. The plot had been carefully laid. If it failed, Don Ernesto would take the whole blame, and, considering himself a martyr, would not divulge the names of those who had backed him. He was the kind of man who would die on the rack without so much as moving his lips. If he succeeded—it meant civil war.

147

"But how did you catch this man? How did—"

Talbot gestured impatiently.

"There's not the time to tell you. 'Tis to be this very morning, and the scoundrel has two loaded pistols."

After the murder, Don Ernesto was to ride to Plymouth on a horse provided for this purpose. Then he was to join his fellow conspirators aboard Tom Gillard's shallop, which was ready to sail at a moment's notice, and they were to carry the news to Spain. Gillard had been bought with Spanish gold and the promise of a Spanish title and estate. He was in the thing up to—and perhaps beyond—his neck.

"At Exeter they told me the Queen had come here. Where is she? In God's name, man, where is she? The guards at the gate thought me mad, and I slipped past them in the confusion."

"But the Queen's safe and well. I saw her with mine own eyes, not ten minutes ago. She's changing her clothes in the chamber beyond that arras over there—"

Talbot glanced wildly at the two open windows. The arras was motionless. To the right, lower, nearer the center of the castle, were two other open windows, smaller ones, uncurtained, disclosing steps. To the left was the sallyport. Talbot saw that the sallyport was unlocked. He wheeled upon the servant, whose mouth was hanging open with amazement.

"Is there no guard at that gate?"

"There—there should be. Aye, 'twas always—"

Talbot ran a few steps toward the gate. He saw the black horse, fresh and fast and thin, with the red Moorish saddle, on the other side of the moat. He could see the device upon that saddle: The sable, a fess wavy argent between two inverted axes proper. He had seen that device before on the left sleeve of Ratface's coat,

148

where every bodyservant wore his master's cognizance.
"Call the guard! Call them out!"

He raced for the small windows. The menial got in
his way, but he knocked the fellow backward with a
blow on the chest. He scrambled through a window,
raced up the steps.

"The guard! Ho, the guard!"

At the head of the steps he found a guardsman. He lay
sprawled on the pavement before a smaller branching
corridor, and blood came in a full, free stream from a
wound in the left side of his neck above the gorget.

Drops of blood led away from this corpse, and down
the small passage. But even without this, it was obvious
that the man had been guarding the entrance of the
small passage. There was a door at the end. Talbot ran
there, burst through, shoved aside an arras—and came
upon the Queen.

"Merciful angels of heaven!"

For all the efforts of poets and court painters to convince a skeptical world, Elizabeth Tudor never had
been beautiful. Now she was within a few weeks of
forty. She stood in the center of the chamber; she was
wigless, unpainted, and garbed only in cotton underclothes.

Talbot stamped to a halt not four feet from her, but
she did not stir, and after that single exclamation she
said not a word. Her head was high, her discolored teeth
bared almost as though in a snarl, but her eyes were
utterly calm, even cold.

She thought, of course, that she was about to be killed.

Of the five tiring-women about her, two ran screaming from the room; two, who had been kneeling, slumped
to sitting positions on the floor and sat, stunned, staring
at the intruder as though at Satan; the fifth unobtrusively
fainted.

149

"Madame—Your Majesty—"

The arras covered the two garden windows stirred at one end. A long blue pistol barrel appeared there, a dark head behind it.

The Queen was nearer to Talbot than was the pistol, so with the quickness of thought he sprang upon the Queen.

A whirring sound, a brief hissing shower of sparks, then a click. The thing had missed fire. It would take several minutes to reprime.

But a second pistol appeared.

Don Ernesto Jesus de Santillana y Canovia had entered by the same door as Talbot, using a key with which he had been provided, and had moved behind the tapestries covering the wall until he had his back to the windows that faced the garden. It was providence that none of the women had seen him.

Another whirr. Another shower of sparks.

Talbot Slanning put both hands on the flat, dry breast of the Defender of the Faith and pushed as hard as he could. She went right over backward, banging the floor with her buttocks.

There was an explosion. On the far side of the room a dozen tiny shards flew in many directions, and a flat chunk of lead dropped with a thud. It must have passed directly between Talbot and the Queen. It was harmless now, on the floor.

Smoke drifted carelessly across the chamber. One of the women started to scream. She screamed as loudly as she could, without words, without sense, and with never a pause.

Talbot, on hands and knees from the force of his own push, saw the tapestry stir again. He sprang to his feet.

Elizabeth of England was flat on her back. She no longer looked like a lioness at bay. She looked only like

150

what she was—a flustered, flabbergasted, middle-aged woman in unbecoming underclothes.

The tiring-woman stopped screaming and toppled in a swoon.

Talbot ran to the tapestry, yanked it with both hands. Its folds fell about his head. He pushed them aside. Before him, at the other end of the garden, men were streaming from the courtyard, waving weapons. Immediately below, rising to his feet, was Don Ernesto Jesus de Santillana y Canovia.

Talbot vaulted the window sill.

Don Ernesto at all costs must be captured alive. Otherwise it would be difficult if not impossible to prove that he, Talbot Slanning, had not had some part in this attempt upon the Queen's life.

The Spaniard slipped through the sallyport, slamming it behind him. That must have been part of the scheme, the bribery, leaving that door unlocked and unguarded for purposes of escape. Talbot wrenched it open, raced out on the bridge.

This footbridge was no more than a temporary thing, put there, assumedly, for the convenience of servants during the extensive preparations that must have preceded the coming of the Queen. It was no more than a single ten-inch plank, about fourteen feet long.

Don Ernesto, at the other bank, wheeled, stooping. He'd heard the pursuit. He grasped the end of the plank. Talbot jumped.

The plank splashed into the moat, but Talbot had landed sprawling upon the edge of the bank, grabbing two handsful of weeds and grasses. He rolled, avoiding a rapier that would have pinned him to the earth. He rose. His own rapier came out.

"So!"

"*Madre de Dios!* You die!"

151

"We'll see about that," said Talbot Slanning.

It was the first time that Talbot actually had looked upon the face of this Don Ernesto Santillana, and the sight was a shock. Here stood a skeleton. The eyes were great black blobs of light set in skin that was pale, brittle as flint, taut as though drawn in pain. The man suffered, surely. He should have been dead. Yet here he was, alive and fighting.

And how he was fighting! Even Talbot backed away from that lunatic rush. But soon Talbot stood.

The men who had swarmed across the garden and who now crowded through the sallygate to pause, baffled, at the edge of the bridgeless moat, for the most part occupied themselves in those few swift moments with shouting for bowmen or trying to salvage the floating plank. A few cool ones merely watched the combat; and these were rewarded by some very pretty swordplay.

Don Ernesto, insane though he might be, though he surely was, and at a glance puny, had muscles from nowhere and a hate-sharpened brain. He moved like a shadow, all nerve and speed, deadly, utterly cold.

Talbot's case was otherwise. He did not wish to kill. He feared this more than he feared the sliver of bright steel that danced before his eyes and licked in and out around his guard. He saw almost instantly that Don Ernesto's breast was protected by a brigandine. That rigidity of the torso, that stiffness when the dagger arm was drawn back, was not wholly accountable to Spanish pride, or to a memory of fencing lessons. No, there was mail under the doublet: Talbot was sure of this. So—a full thrust for the heart or lungs might have meant a snapped blade, and death.

But Talbot had no thought of thrusting anyway. This man must live! The throat was unprotected, as were the eyes; but these Talbot avoided, and he worked for the right arm only.

Maniacs have a vitality that comes from God knows where. Four times Talbot reached the upper right arm with short hard cuts, and twice his point snicked briefly into the forearm. But still Don Ernesto fought on. Nor was he wild! He was savage, but swift, alert, making no unnecessary move.

A long desperate thrust slid through the flesh of Talbot's left armpit. It stung. Exasperated, he stepped in, cutting open the Spaniard's left cheek. Blood splattered like rain in springtime. The man would collapse yet. He *had* to collapse! Madman or no, he could not keep up this pace much longer.

It was only a matter of seconds anyway. Neither would remain alive when the bowmen came, or when guardsmen, running out of the main gate and around the castle, reached them back here. They would be cut to pieces without question. For it was a time when men did not stop to ask questions. The Queen's life had been attempted.

Don Ernesto disengaged twice, raised his guard, swept into a beautiful long lunge for the heart. It was as swift as light. Talbot caught it barely in time, and raised the blade, straightening his sword arm. But he could not divert his own point: he wasn't given a chance. And Don Ernesto, coming in, spitted himself upon Talbot's blade, which slipped without a sound through his throat and came out red, a full four inches, at the back of his neck.

Don Ernesto fell instantaneously, indisputably dead.

CHAPTER SEVENTEEN

Talbot stepped back, coughing, choking with rage. His muscles were all too well trained; his reflexes, alas, had been exact, unfailing. He had done what he ought not to have done.

A quarrel struck his left arm, whirling him around. He fell to his knees, cursing. When he got up an arrow thumped into the ground where he had been. Another flew past his face.

The bowmen had arrived. They were shooting across the moat. And around a corner of Powderham Castle came men who waved pikes and swords.

No, assuredly there would not be time for considered questions and answers. Talbot would have preferred to pause, to explain. But his first instinct was to dodge death, which advanced swiftly toward where he stood. The black Neopolitan mare, admirably disciplined, had not stirred throughout this fight. It was neither hobbled nor tethered. Scorning a stirrup, Talbot vaulted into the red saddle and was off.

There were two musket explosions.

An arrow glanced against the mare's neck, raising a welt, but that brought about no break in her stride. She

154

swerved only for an instant. An exquisite beast she was, the fastest that Talbot ever had known.

He leaned low. There was a great clamor behind him, but the road ahead lay smooth, even.

He had ridden for fully two miles before it came to him that he was going north, toward Exeter, away from Plymouth. But Plymouth was the place he wished to go. For Ratface was in Plymouth, and so was Tom Gillard and the associates of Gillard. These men he'd confront, and he would cause their arrest before he himself submitted. Without them he was lost.

The mare ran swiftly, smoothly. Talbot swerved to the left at the first lane, and soon he was galloping across the moor. He knew every inch of this country. It was possible, he estimated, by going through or near Chudleigh, and under the shadow of Rippon Tor, close to Newton Abbot and Dean Prior, he might reach Plymouth ahead of such of those at Powderham who proved quick-witted enough to realize that he would make for that port. The road by way of Torquay, along the shore, was better, but longer.

After a while he veered a little left again, for the thought had come to him that by going this far west he might give pursuers the notion that he was making for Chagford, and this would mean that they'd annoy Katherine. He *heard* no pursuers: he just took them for granted.

It was about noon when, somewhere near Ashburton, he drew rein at a peasant's hut.

"Wine, man! I'll pay well!"

The peasant had no wine.

"Ale, then, in God's name!"

The lout had no ale either, or beer.

"Oh, give me water, even!"

This in time was provided, though he had to drink it

out of a leather bucket that smelled like the floor of a horse stall.

"Yuh—yuh ride on the Queen's business?"

Talbot nodded grimly.

"Aye," he said.

He heard the sound of hoofs, from the north. He looked at the peasant.

"Hast sharp ears? Is that one horse only, as I think?"

"Aye, your worship. One horse."

Talbot pursed his lips, staring at the black mare. She had run marvelously well, and had a great heart; given even a short rest, she would run well again; but to push her now, might be to kill her. He led her around to the back of the hut, where he drew sword and dagger, the peasant's eyes popping.

"Heed me! If this man rides past I'll not stir. But if he pauses, keep out of our way!"

The hoofbeats came nearer. They slowed as they approached the hut, and Talbot took a better grip on his dagger. Then the horseman started to canter. But directly the other side of the hut he came to a stop. Talbot heard a creak of leather, the scuff of feet, and then a voice he knew so well:

"Ho, fellow! Hast seen a young madcap ride past here on a black steed with a high red saddle, eh?"

Talbot ran round a corner of the hut.

"Captain Drake! Whatever make you here?"

"Slanning, lad! Are you safe?"

It was embarrassing for both of them. They embraced, but with forced carelessness. They drank water together, wincing. They splashed the rest of the water upon their tired steeds. And all the while they talked, jabbering like a couple of schoolgirls.

"You're making for Plymouth?"

"Aye. I went north a little first."

156

"I slipped away in the fuss. I took it to be my part to gallop for Plymouth and Ned Crocker there, and this prisoner of Crocker's of whom you'd told me. Then even if they overtook you I might be able to prove your innocence."

"Unless they'd killed me first. But, thanks, my friend. You know Ned Crocker, then?"

"Who doesn't?"

He rapped a knobby forefinger against Talbot Slanning's chest.

"But *there's* just the trouble, mind you, lad."

"I don't see . . ."

"Who *doesn't* known Ned Crocker? Certainly Tom Gillard does, to mention only one."

"Aye, Tom Gillard," Talbot said slowly.

"Gillard will miss this Spanish servant. But he saw you—had a glimpse of your face, you said?"

"Oh, yes."

"Then don't you think he'll know where to look?"

"He's a Queen's prisoner," Talbot was quick to point out, "and he's not supposed to put a foot on shore."

"Why, so are you. And neither were you. Yet—here you are."

"Um . . ."

"If that Spanish servant blabs, then what would become of Master Thomas Gillard?"

"Aye."

"My hope is that we'll get there first."

He put a hand on Talbot's arm.

"For mark, ye, Slanning, on that servant's tale all our safety hangs."

"*Our* safety?"

"Oh, 'tis mine as well. The Spaniards have her ear now, and she must heed 'em whether she will or no. Should it seem as though one of my own ship's company, one of my closest companions, was involved in a plot upon the Queen's life, why, what would happen to Francis Drake?"

This of course was true, transparently so. It was as Talbot had told Katherine Abergavenny: Drake could not *afford* to stand by and see Talbot disgraced.

"Yet if we can prove 'twas all a Spanish plot—as we can do through this servant—then will I become a patriot and no pirate, and then we'll each get our share of that treasure, and we'll win the Queen's gracious permission to make another voyage to the New World soon."

Talbot grinned.

"Another voyage . . . the Southern Sea, eh?"

"The Southern Sea, lad! And the gold we've seen these past few months will be floor-sweepings to what we'll pluck there!"

They mounted and were off. They did not talk, but rode hard. For a mariner, unexpectedly, Francis Drake was a good horseman, by no means graceful, but dogged. undeviating.

There was only one brief pause. Fairly within sight of the steeple of St. Andrew's, six men sprang into their path, grabbing the reins of both steeds. These men held bludgeons.

"Your purses, my fine lords!"

Talbot reached for his sword. Francis Drake, furious at the delay, roared in rage, "Robber, eh?" and drew and fired a small pistol. A man fell, shot in the groin, screaming. The others stumbled back.

"Robbers, eh? Come on, Slanning!"

They rode on.

Nobody turned to stare at them as they cantered into old Plymouth town. There was no stir, no gossip, to suggest that the news from Powderham Castle had reached this place.

Yet it was impossible to believe that the Spaniards had not posted at least one lookout at Powderham to insure that word be sent to Plymouth in the event that the plan miscarried. Such a messenger of course would do nothing to raise an alarm: he would report only to his masters.

Talbot and Captain Drake went to the back of Ned Crocker's wineship, and gave the signal-knock. They received no answer.

Drake shifted from foot to foot, regularly, unthinkingly, but his face was as grave as that of any person. Talbot too was frankly worried. He wetted his lips nervously. He straightened his ruff.

They knocked again. Still no answer.

Talbot tried the door, and it opened in his hand. This in itself was strange, and ominous. The street door of Ned Crocker's wineshop, the front door, all day and every day excepting the Sabbath, and much of the night as well, was kept open, or at least unlocked. The shop in truth did a very good legitimate business. But the back door, the one that opened into this alley, Crocker always kept carefully bolted.

They drew their swords before they went in. They went directly to a room upstairs, a room that overlooked the Barbican, the same in which Talbot and Robert Butterwalk had waited for the completion of the negotiations with Captain Vaarts. It was there that Ned Crocker was to have stayed with his prisoner.

Nor had Crocker quit the place. He lay on the floor, face-down, the back of his head a red mass. The blood was beginning to dry around the edges, and blood dries very quickly.

Of Ratface the only sign was a length of cord cut in many places.

On the floor was a coin, a Spanish eight-real piece,

glittering bravely in that otherwise dim place. Spanish coins of course were no novelty anywhere in England, least of all in the bustling port of Plymouth. It was here that much of the wine trade with Spain had centered for so many years, and where also many a pirate was wont to sell his booty and to buy supplies. Spanish gold was good gold anywhere in the world, accepted currency, the stablest, not subject to the chipping from below and sudden fluctuations of value from above that too often marked the English coins. Reals and half-reals, escudos, pieces-of-eight, maravedis, castellanos, all were common sights along the Barbican. But most of them had come a long way, often enough an exceedingly rough way as well, and they were nicked, scratched, battered, the milled edges worn. The coin on the floor at Ned Crocker's, a maravedi, was Spanish gold at its best: bright, unthumbed, as though it had just come from the mint at Seville.

The Captain toed it thoughtfully. No more than Talbot did he make any move to pick it up.

"So Tom Gillard *did* know where to look!" he whispered.

"Come on," said Talbot.

They hurried downstairs. They left their horses, preferring to wriggle and squirm through the crowd the short distance to the quay, where they stood a while watching the sails of the Gillard shallop slowly and tantalizingly fill, as she moved out of the Catwater toward the open sound.

"She's fast. What will overhaul her?"

Francis Drake looked around. Better than any man alive, perhaps, he knew the shipping of Plymouth harbor. From the top of a mast here, a sharply steeved bowsprit there, a peaked yardarm, the merest corner of a square tuck, an overhanging stern-castle gleaming with tiny square windows—from these things, at a glance, he knew the ship and remembered her capabilities, could calculate how much time it would take to get her outside.

"There must be *one* vessel!"

"There is one, and only one," Francis Drake said. " 'Twas made by the Spaniards themselves, too. There's irony for you, Slanning."

"You don't mean—"

" 'Tis a shade heavy in the water just now, but for all of that I'll warrant it will overtake anything afloat in this harbor. And if the sheriff's men and the Queen's commissioners who are aboard of her will not listen to our words—on my conscience, Slanning, lad, we'll talk to them in a louder language!"

CHAPTER EIGHTEEN

Guardsmen had swept into Chagford like a gale from
the sea, and they swarmed over Abergavenny Manor.
Katherine, frightened but calm, stood in the center of the
entrance-hall and for some time tried in vain to get an
explanation of this business. The guardsman surrounded
her, shouted questions, dashed away before she had a
chance to answer them—only to come back, an instant
later, with further questions.

There was no politeness in these soldiers. This was a
national emergency, and they were privileged seekers.
There could be no danger of treading on the wrong toes.
Besides, who was this country girl, alone in an old manor
house? What possible court connections could she have?

The one thing that Katherine was able to learn,
promptly and unmistakably, was that these men sought
Talbot. Talbot, she gathered, was believed to be the head
of a gigantic conspiracy to overthrow the throne, to kill
Elizabeth herself, to kill also Hatton, Leicester, Cecil,
Sussex, to place Mary of Scotland upon the throne. It was
a French plot, some said. Most of the court, however,
were convinced that it was a Spanish plot. All were
agreed that Talbot Slanning was its genius. He had slain

two men and had endeavored to kidnap the Queen's own person. He had knocked the Queen down.

"No!" cried Katherine.

He had knocked the Queen down, truly. And he had escaped. Riding in this direction.

"Where is he? Where have you hidden him?"

Katherine stood very still, looking taller than she was, and her hazel eyes held only scorn. She sniffed.

"I do not know where Talbot Slanning is," she said.

"You've hidden him! He rode this way! Where is he?"

Katherine started: "Say now, if mayhap you'd give me a chance to—"

The captain of the guardsmen cried: "This Master Slanning, he was your lover, was he not?"

"He was my betrothed."

"He was your lover," the captain rasped. "No banns were posted. There's been no betrothal."

"There'd been no time," Katherine countered. "We had planned—"

"And then Master Slanning murdered Sir Francis Monckton, eh? Aye, 'tis well remembered, I can promise that."

For a little while after that the captain of the guardsmen did not disturb her but busied himself directing the search. Not only the house but all the outbuildings as well, and the grounds, were tramped over again and again. Tapestries were yanked from the walls. Every room, every closet, was entered. Katherine's own wardrobe was spread upon the floor, as though the soldiers expected to find Talbot Slanning hidden in the folds of one of her gowns.

The captain strode back to the hall.

"You know where this man is."

"I do not."

163

"You've not seen him? He has not been here since his return with that pirate, Drake?"

Katherine did not hesitate. Normally there was no woman more truthful and frank. But where Talbot was concerned there was for Katherine Abergavenny only one truth, which was Talbot's safety.

"I have not seen him since he left these parts," she said.

The captain was a black-bearded fellow of truculent appearance, not really bad-hearted, not professionally and habitually a bully, but just now convinced that only aggressiveness would serve to find the man he must have. He loved and feared his Queen, for he was a good subject, and he knew his duty.

"You're lying," he said.

He gripped her arm with big bruising fingers, and marched her toward the staircase.

"You'll remain in your own bedchamber until we have completed the search, and then if we have found nothing we'll return to question you. It won't be long," he added glumly, "and the questioning will not be tender. This is high treason, my fine lady."

When he had locked her in, she hesitated not a moment. She did not know where Talbot was, but she knew that Captain Drake's ships lay in the Catwater at Plymouth; and she knew—for Talbot himself had told her—that Drake would protect him.

To her Drake was a pirate, a desperate, murdering, thieving adventurer of the sea; but if Talbot trusted him, Katherine would trust him too.

The key had scarcely turned in the lock when she was at the window and testing the trellis upon which honeysuckle grew. Once this trellis had made her a perfect ladder. She had not been on it since her early teens. It was older now, and she herself heavier; yet she clambered out on it without a qualm.

It held.

She ran around to the front of the house, keeping as much as she could to the shelter of the rose bushes, though they tore her gown.

There were seven horses, all saddled, none tethered, and a single, half-asleep groom. Katherine ran toward them—ran fast but silently. She knew horses. Instinctively she selected the swiftest of these beasts; and her foot scarcely touched the stirrup as she mounted.

The groom yelled. Somebody came running out of the house. But by that time Katherine was halfway down Abergavenny Lane.

At the mouth of the lane was a sentry. He had drawn a broadsword when he heard the shouts from the manor house, but the last thing he expected was a pretty girl in black velvet, riding low and hard. He gawped. As she flashed past him he tried to grab the reins, and failing in this he slashed at the horse's rump. Both actions were tardy. Katherine was riding away.

There was no notable evidence of excitement in Plymouth when she arrived. She had herself rowed out to the disputed Spanish fregata. The boatman was amazed, but obedient. He knew a lady when he saw one.

The sheriff, large, fat, worried, was too kind a man actually to refuse her admittance to the cabin, but he explained that Captain Drake was not aboard, and that the vessel was in official custody.

"But I must set this Drake. Tell me, does he return soon?"

"Nay, I know not that. He's been summoned to attend the Queen's Majesty at Powderham, and sometimes she takes a long while calling men in. But whether he comes back or no, you must not remain in this ship, ma'am."

He was pushing her gently toward the ladder, at the foot of which the hired boatman waited. All about them was the bang of Plymouth harbor, the clank and clatter of docks less than two hundred yards away.

Katherine, wild, tried one more chance.

"Is Master Talbot Slanning aboard then, pray?"

Now the sheriff's hand tightened upon her arm, and his eyes became small and thoughtful, searching. Two of his deputies approached, and they too were staring curiously at Katherine.

"Nay, ma'am, and what do you know of Master Slanning?"

"Is he aboard, I asked. I'd speak to him."

"Why, so would I."

The sheriff belched thoughtfully.

"Do you know where he's been these twelve hours past?" he asked.

"I know that he's—"

Katherine stopped, for the grip on her arm had become painfully tight.

"Nay," she said simply. "I have no knowledge of him."

Lacking practice, she was a poor liar. The sheriff nodded meaningfully. Then he waved away the boatman, and led Katherine to the stern cabin, a small but richly furnished place. He closed the door.

"Ma'am," he said solemnly, "this is the Queen's business, and I am the Queen's agent in Devonshire. You must answer my questions with the truth or you may become a party to high treason. I know from your face that you have some knowledge of Talbot Slanning's whereabouts. My position and it could be my very life are at stake. I'm indisposed to be gentle."

She tried a smile, which faded fast.

"I tell you, I do not know where he is."

166

"Where *has* he been, then? Where was he yesternight? He surely did not slip out of here in order to play a game of bowls on the Hoe?"

"Nay, I—I know not."

He came very close to her. He was a good man, the sheriff, by no means young, a man of religious feeling, a father, naturally reluctant to use violence upon a female of good family. But since dawn he had been twisted with anxiety about the location of his most important prisoner. He knew the importance of Talbot Slanning to the court, and he dreaded to think of the punishment he himself faced if Slanning was not returned to custody.

"Ma'am, I have three deputies aboard of this vessel, and two Queen's commissioners beside, who are here to keep an eye on the treasure that's in the hold. These men are under my command. They know that the situation is serious. The crew can do nothing, I've sent all their weapons ashore. Below, besides the gold and pearls, there is a cell with leg irons and wrist irons, and nobody can hear any noises that might be made in that cell. You'll go there, ma'am, at this very instant, and my men will go with you to beat you and twist your arm unless you talk honestly with me here and now."

Katherine shook her head.

She whispered: "I do not know where he is."

The sheriff took her by the hand.

"Come," he said sadly.

167

CHAPTER NINETEEN

Hurried steps sounded upon the deck. The door flew open, and a short, dusty, red-bearded young man burst into the cabin. He paid not the slightest attention to Katherine, but addressed himself to the sheriff.

"Ask me not why I do this, for there's no time to tell you, Dick," he said. "Tom Gillard's shallop is making for the open sea, and this is the only vessel in the whole harbor that could catch her. There are Spaniards in that shallop who must be brought back, alive! We sail, Dick."

"Frank, you're mad! The Queen's business—"

" 'Tis the Queen's business on which we sail. Nay, I'll brook no pause. Step out on deck and—"

"The treasure! You're trying to take it to France!"

"Fool! I could have done that earlier, without ever returning to England with it, if I'd so wished. I tell you, Dick, we chase that shallop. Come."

"Nay, I'll not permit such folly. I'll not—"

The Captain whipped out a pistol. It was not loaded, but the sheriff didn't know that, and neither did Katherine Abergavenny.

The sheriff said nothing. His mouth fell open, and his eyes grew large. His whole body stiffened. But he had known Francis Drake from boyhood: the man wouldn't ever utter an idle threat.

"I'll not be stopped, Dick, even by a Queen's sheriff. Unstrap that sword-belt."

A moment later he was following the sheriff out to the deck—following him close, with the pistol pressed against the small of the sheriff's back. And Katherine heard him saying: "I'll take the swords of your men, too, since these are the only weapons your diligence has left us here. Command it."

A few minutes after this, Katherine, ignored, still standing in the cabin as if stunned, heard the shrilling of a whistle, then Captain Drake's voice:

"Yonkers aloft! You at the bow, bring the cable to the capstern and break out the anchor. Yonkers! Let fall the foresail, cut 'er away. Spread the sprit. Let fall the main course. You forward, bring over that shank painter and cat the anchor. Hi, *are ye lame?* Aloft, break out bonnets and dablers."

El Draque, the dragon, was in motion. Katherine, bewildered, frightened, started for the cabin door. It was opened, and Talbot Slanning came in.

The shallop, *Gillard's Pride,* owed her reputation for speed less to rig and canvas, of which she carried but little, than to her narrow beam, her lightness, her sweet handling qualities. She could yaw at amazing angles, sailing almost into the teeth of the wind, yet she was a hard vessel to handle when the seas were running high. She didn't pitch much, but she was a prodigious roller. Were it not for the sharply steved bowsprit, her prow would have resembled that of a galley, and it was much too low to permit the use of a spritsail, even in fine weather. She carried no tops, and her foresail and main course, even when supplemented by bonnets, were not large. Her mizzen was lateen rigged.

She resembled a Mediterranean pirate galley, indeed, in more ways than one. For example, her lightness and narrow beam made heavy cannon inadvisable, and she carried, in addition to a few hand-pieces, only two stern culverins, not large ones, and a falconet forward for chasing. Gillard relied upon her speed and the ferocity of her crew in boarding.

"We'll overhaul before dark," Drake predicted. " 'Twill be buckier when we get past Redding Point, and perhaps it'll wet our spritsail, but that should make the handling harder for Tom Gillard."

He roared down the deck: "Yonkers below! Lace those dablers tighter! I'll have every inch of spread we can crack on!"

Mariners were coiling the anchor cable, stowing the ship's boat, running up pennants, tightening leech-lines. Not a one stopped to ask what all this was about. Two Queen's commissioners and three sheriffs had been overpowered and disarmed, and the ship was sailing in direct violation of the Queen's command, as every one of the men knew; but they trusted Francis Drake. They had been away from their homes for fourteen months, having passed through unbelievable hardships; and when they'd returned to Plymouth they were not permitted to go ashore and get drunk, or even to receive visitors. Within the very sight of their sweethearts and wives they'd been obliged to remain aboard, trusting blindly to the Captain. Now the Captain was roaring commands from the half-deck, and again they were headed fair toward the open sea—for what? And where? Why? They didn't know. But they did as they were told, and did it swiftly and well.

"You don't think a man like Tom Gillard will strike without resistance?" asked Oxenham. "You don't think we'll have to fight?"

"Oho! We'll fight! Be sure of that!"

"With what?"

170

"Eh?"

"What weapons'll we use? Whilst you were at Powderham, sir, the high sheriff ordered all gunpowder and sidearms ashore. Must we prevail over this mess of Channel scum with naught but our good Devonshire fists?"

Captain Drake showed no astonishment at this news.

"There are worse weapons," he said equably. "Besides, it may be that Tom Gillard doth not know this."

"Ah, but he does know it. Everybody in Plymouth knows it, for the taking of the arms ashore caused great talk. Hundreds watched. Gillard himself watched, from his own poop."

"Ah, well . . . There's my sword, and Slanning's, together with the daggers. And there are four rapiers we took from the sheriff and his men. And there are the capstern bars. And we can tear down the partition in the forecastle to make clubs with. Also, you should never forget, John," he added gently, "that God is on our side."

"Aye."

"And there's Slanning's skill. You know as well as I do, John, that with a rapier Talbot Slanning's worth any three."

He looked around.

"But where makes our fencing master, eh?"

"In your cabin. You sent him there for something."

The Captain nodded, remembering. Ah, yes. There had been a woman in the cabin—a curious thing, for he never permitted women in his ships, even for ceremonial occasions. He'd had no time to ask about her then; and not until later, on the half-deck with the ship already under way, did he think of her. He'd sent Slanning to learn who she was and what in the name of the devil she was doing aboard *El Draque*. And Slanning had not yet returned.

"Shall I go after him?"

171

"Nay, I'll go myself. Linger here and watch that none lags."

On the way to his own cabin, the Captain stopped before the trussed-up sheriff and commissioners.

"There'll be battle soon. I'll have you removed for safety."

The high sheriff said gravely: "You'll regret this, Frank, for the rest of your life."

The Captain shrugged.

"If I must needs regret it," he said, "then the rest of my life will not be a long time anyway."

He had not known what to expect when he entered his cabin a moment later, but surely not the sight of Talbot Slanning, glum and silent, with feet spread, frowning at the floor, while there faced him one of the most startling dark beauties it ever had been Francis Drake's privilege to see. The girl was tallish, supple of build, with hazel eyes that were crammed with seriousness.

Captain Drake bowed deeply before her. He knew at a glance that she was a lady; and he rather prided himself upon his bow, practiced for many long hours in this very cabin.

Talbot Slanning blurted: "We must turn back."

"Are you mad? There's a fair full wind, and near the Bolts the sea'll be rough enough so that Gillard will not dare to make many yaws in that slim craft. He's half caught already."

"We must turn back," Talbot repeated. He motioned toward the girl. "This—this is my betrothed, sir—Mistress Katherine Abergavenny of Abergavenny Manor. I've caused her too much trouble already, and I'll not be taking her into the fight we'd have ahead of us if we overhaul Tom Gillard."

The Captain bowed again at the mention of Katherine's name. He had heard of her, knew her lineage.

"At the very least," Talbot pursued, "Katherine must be put ashore at Stoke point or thereabouts."

The Captain said quietly: "If we did that, the Spaniards would escape with the coming of night."

"Then they must escape. My betrothed must not—"

Katherine Abergavenny cut in: "You speak much of your betrothed. D'ye think I'd remain the betrothed of one who runs away from a fight?"

Talbot swallowed hard, staring at her. He had never heard her speak like this. Her voice was icy, slow, precise.

"The lady says well," Francis Drake ventured.

Talbot wheeled upon him. Talbot Slanning was the court ruffler again, an angry man with hand on swordhilt.

"Nay, no man shall call me a coward! Lug it out, sir!"

The Captain put a hand on Talbot's right arm. He said softly: "My friend—my friend."

Katherine's voice remained as cold as before.

"Must you brawl in my presence also, in a try to assert your sorry manhood? Must you learn politeness as well as courage from your admiral?"

She addressed herself to Drake, and her voice softened.

"I have heard much of Francis Drake, and that he is a valiant admiral and general. No fool, too, they tell me. So there'll be fighting?"

"Aye, ma'am, there will be fighting."

Katherine's head was high.

"And where best could I view it?"

The Captain glanced once, very briefly, at Talbot Slanning, who stood taut, red, his whole frame trembling. For an instant the Captain was almost afraid of this man. He'd seen him in battle.

173

Then the Captain looked again at Katherine Abergavenny.

"Methinks the half-deck, ma'am. It's higher."

"My thanks to you, sir."

She dropped him a curtsey, and he bowed.

"But keep clear of the man at the jackstaff, ma'am."

"That I shall certainly do."

She went out, with no nod to Talbot.

The two men faced one another.

When Captain Drake broke the silence the voice that had sent oaken seamen flying was most amazingly soft.

"Slanning, you're a fool. And the lady's right. The business we make now is the Queen's and England's, and 'tis not a time for any private notions of honor. Nobody ever called you a coward, not even Mistress Abergavenny, who only tried to taunt you out of your silliness. Not a coward, no. But a fool."

Abruptly he fell to his knees and began to pray. He prayed for Talbot, for Katherine, and for the safety of the Queen's Majesty; and he prayed also for England.

Talbot was thinking wildly: *I never turned from peril when the peril was only mine, but God, oh my God, if Katherine ever should be hurt!*

The voice continued, sure, firm, yet humble. Awkwardly Talbot got to his own knees, bowed his own head. And after a time the voice ceased, and Talbot, not looking up, muttered, "Amen." He heard the Captain rise, felt a hand on his shoulder.

"It will be your own fight, lad. For I appoint you now to command the attack. Pray, man, pray! Pray for the help of the Lord, God of Hosts, and afterward go up on deck and buss your beloved and draw your sword and fight like Hell!"

The wind held, and they rode firm and free very close

174

to Staddon Point. There wasn't a cloud in the sky, though the sea was making up. It was late afternoon.

"Three full hours of daylight," muttered Tom Moone.

Talbot came out of the cabin, blinking a little. Katherine Abergavenny stood at the rail near him, her face turned away.

Dead ahead, flying like a thing frightened, was the *Gillard's Pride*.

It gave Talbot a start to see how close they were to *Gillard's Pride*. Scarcely more than half a mile away, and drawing nearer all the time.

He came up behind Katherine, who must have known he was there, and he said hesitantly:

"I—I'm sorry. Only it had seemed to me that maybe—well, if thou'rt with child—"

She turned, and he saw that she had been weeping.

"Oh, I do love thee so, my sweet!"

She made a curious little sound in her throat, and without any hesitation or shame threw both arms around his neck.

"Oh, Talbot!"

Somewhere in the lower shrouds a seaman snickered. Francis Drake blew his whistle.

"Lace that bonnet tighter, ye beefwit! There'll be time enough for entertainment when we get ashore, unless you want to wake up with sand in your ears!"

Presently Talbot stood before the Captain again. Half playfully, half seriously he touched his hat.

"Your worship?"

"Eh?"

"A duty for me?"

"Nay, I've already appointed you to a duty. I'll overhaul yonder vessel and *you'll* see that she's taken. All the men are at your command for this, once the ships have kissed."

175

Talbot bounded to the waist. He felt as he'd felt before, in the wild Americas, when a rare fight was threatening. He laughed as he moved, and laughed as he issued loud orders.

The screens in the waist were fixed to his satisfaction, and water barrels and sand buckets stood everywhere. Since there could be so few actual members of the crew engaged in combat, because there were so few weapons, he had more men to work with in the arrangement of the prosaic details. The sturdy little *El Draque* could not have been better prepared for battle had she been about to face the whole Spanish fleet.

Nobody was permitted aloft, but boys and yonkers were stationed behind the protection of the screens with extra lines for the hasty mending of rig, jury jobs. The six-armed grapnel at the bowsprit was sharpened, and grappling rope and irons were brought to all starboard parts of the vessel above decks.

"We'll take them head-on and then swing broadside starboard," Talbot decided. "Can you manage that, Captain?"

"It will be done, sir."

Aboard of *Gillard's Pride* a culverin coughed white smoke, and a ball whistled athwart *El Draque's* bows.

The other culverin coughed, and part of the larboard rail was carried away at the bow, spewing the air with splinters. No one was hurt. Talbot had long before ordered everybody off the forward deck—except himself.

"She'll speak angrier than that before she makes us worry," he laughed.

The distance now was scarcely three hundred yards. Talbot could see men reloading the culverins, while other men rollered the falconet aft. He caught sight of torches being carried to the tiny fighting tower. Fire-arrows.

176

"Yonkers aloft!" he roared over his left shoulder. "Aloft with water! Wet every line!"

A ball shrieked past his head. He smiled, and quietly descended to the waist. It was time for even him to get under cover. He went to the Captain.

"Can we furl yet?"

The Captain shook his head.

"She'll try some tricks. She's caught, and they know it, but she'll try to dodge and squirm till darkness. We need every inch of canvas."

"It's fire I fear," Talbot explained. "Send me word when we can furl, eh?"

He raised his head, blew a whistle.

"Yonkers below! Refill the water barrels!"

He saw Tom Gillard on the poop of the shallop, and even above the clamor of voices he was able to hear Gillard's commands. He turned. Behind him, high on the half-deck, Katherine Abergavenny was leaning forward, her hair blowing, her cheeks bright red in the breeze. When she caught his eye she waved and smiled.

Gillard's Pride endeavored to yaw, but the persistent fregata followed the movement. Gillard tried another yaw, to starboard, and this time he went too far. The shallop rocked and shivered like a wounded beast; and a sea broke clear across her, carrying away the lateen.

El Draque came around more slowly. Francis Drake was not a man to be shaken off by sea tricks, howsoever wily.

"Heed the forward rigging!"

Wooden-feathered bolts with forked heads were whistling above, and *El Draque's* shrouds were being cut. A yardarm swung crazily. The main topsail flapped and snapped in impotent protest and appeared to be trying to recover its balance. Rope-ends fell thuddingly to the deck.

Aboard the *Gillard's Pride* men were stuffing oil-soaked rags into the tri-spaces of their fire-arrows, igniting them at a cresset that flamed and spluttered in the waist, and shooting them. They hissed furiously through the air, black smoke trailing them, and thunked into the deck of the fregata, into the rails, the masts, and yards. Mariners everywhere were spilling water and throwing sand.

Suddenly everything became quiet. Each man, as though he understood what was happening, ceased his yells, trussed up his points, made ready.

Gillard's Pride had striven too hard to wriggle away. Her smashed mizzen prevented Tom Gillard from bringing her about to meet the attack head-on. Now she floundered like a beached fish. And *El Draque's* prow moved relentlessly to catch her on the starboard quarter.

Francis Drake, having obeyed orders, quit the jackstaff, and as he drew sword and dagger and ran for the waist, his voice boomed across the empty sea:

"Take the ship, Master Slanning! She's yours!"

Talbot was ready. Six swords with daggers, four capstern bars, an array of improvised clubs—but he knew his men. These were the same lads who had been lost to panic on a certain memorable morning at Nombre de Dios, but since that time they had indeed learned to fight. He looked around, smiling. The men were silent, expressionless, as they watched the vessels come closer.

From the half-deck Katherine Abergavenny waved to Talbot, and he flourished his rapier in reply.

The crash was terrific, throwing them off their feet. It seemed for an instant that the shallop would be cut fairly in two. The six long spikes of *El Draque's* grapnel thundered and screeched through her deck cabin amidships, carried away a long portion of her rail, and sent her splinter-pocked crewmen scampering for safety. Timbers

178

made a hideous protest. Captain Drake roared a command to the mariner who had replaced him at the jackstaff, and the fregata was swung neatly, confidently, stern to larboard. Her waist nudged the violated waist of *Gillard's Pride*. That is, the vessels kissed.

Talbot called: "Hooks! Hooks and chains!"

Somebody fired a musket. One of the culverins coughed yet again. A man near Talbot turned around twice, knelt on the deck, and then quietly collapsed, half rolling over on his back. There was a startled, somewhat puzzled expression on his face, and blood leapt from his mouth. Another seaman instantly seized this fellow's capstern bar, for Talbot had arranged an unarmed but alert reserve.

"Hooks!"

The grappling lines were thrown, not in a shower but now by a man at one end of the waist, now by a man at the other, and again by one in the middle. Muskets banged on the forward deck of *Gillard's Pride*. The men in the fighting tower, which had sagged under the shock, nevertheless continued to rain down bolts and quarrels.

The grappling chains were drawn. The vessels ground and shrieked together, screaming as though in pain.

They showed alone upon a rough but not unfriendly sea, those vessels. They had that part of the Channel to themselves—and to the setting sun.

They rose and shudderingly fell, while a hazy blue sky, close and cloudless, serenely watched. The breeze had hushed itself almost into silence, and far to the north England was a gray-purple smear.

"Boarders!"

Talbot sprang from behind the protection of the fighting screen.

"Boarders, follow me!"

He jumped.

179

CHAPTER TWENTY

Because the fregata was so low in the water her waist was about on a level with the overall decks of the shallop. However, she had a beamy tumbledown—for in spite of the bow grapnel she'd been designed as a stand-off fighter—so that the rails of the two vessels were not in contact. The distance was about five feet. Talbot fell to one knee, and put his right fist to the deck to recover his balance. He parried a cutlass blow with his dagger as he did this, and an instant later he was on his feet. The man with the cutlass backed away.

Talbot slipped past a pike, bending his knees. His rapier licked in and out—and then there was no pike.

The man with the cutlass, reinforced by two companions similarly armed, stepped forward again. For a moment Talbot could do nothing but hold them off, parrying with both his blades, not trying to attack. Then he sensed the Captain by his side, and another rapier flashed with his.

He grinned and waded in.

There was little room for swordplay here among the massed wreckage of the cabin, for the long angry splinters of wood were as dangerous as any steel. Talbot and

Francis Drake pushed forward, step by slow step, slashing, jabbing. They did not dare to turn their heads in order to learn whether others had followed them. If not, if they were alone, they could not possibly survive.

But others were coming, struggling there, filling in. As the space broadened, more men were able to dispute passage to a clear deck. When one of these came too eagerly Talbot's rapier slipped between his ribs. The fellow fell, but he fell forward, and as he did so he grabbed one of Francis Drake's ankles. The Captain lurched heavily against Talbot, who was pushed sideways against the wall of the cabin.

This threw his point out of line, and Gillard's men sprang in.

Talbot was cool about it. He had never enjoyed a fight so much. His palm was out; his blade was in a high line, as though it were a saber. The place rang like a blacksmith's shop. But—Captain Drake was down.

At least one of the blows in that rush must have carried past Talbot's guard, though he was not aware of it at the time; for suddenly he knew that he had dropped his dagger and that his left arm swung at his side without feeling—he couldn't lift it.

He brought his right shoulder forward, and advanced his right foot, turning his body a trifle. He moved ahead warily. The grip of his sword was almost motionless, but the point whisked back and forth in small arcs, threatening now an eye, now a mouth, and once it snipped the end off a nose . . .

They didn't like that. Talbot could not attack at the moment, but he was scaring them. They wavered.

Talbot edged forward, keen, catlike, his point never still.

The captain was up again, and his rapier flashed at Talbot's left. Somebody else had moved up on Talbot's right. Talbot could not swivel his eyes to see who this was, but from the shortness of the reach, he took it to be Ellis Hixom, a stumpy man.

From the poop Tom Gillard's voice came:

"*Away, blades! Aloft, aloft!*"

Talbot sensed the trick. With a pause in the resistance, these outnumbered boarders naturally would stop for a moment to settle their position, check their neighbors, catch their breath. But when the boarders stepped back, the bowmen above would have clear targets.

So Talbot didn't pause.

"*'Ware the arrows! 'Ware above!*"

A mariner of Gillard's, startled at the pursuit, which he had not expected, turned, raising his blade. Then he decided not to stand, but to flee. He was late with that decision. Talbot's blade flashed past his guard and sank into the softness of his throat. The mariner's head plopped forward as though he had been hit from behind, and he fell with a crash to his knees, where he swayed a moment, grotesquely upright, the caricature of a man at prayer, before he toppled sideways and was still.

"*The mast! To the mast!*"

A quarrel clanged upon Talbot's helmet, dizzying him for an instant. Still, he reached the mainmast a leap ahead of Hixom and Captain Drake. And there they turned, safe from above.

Stout Tom Moone, bellowing with excitement, charged through a shower of arrows and quarrels, and incredibly was untouched when he reached the shelter of the mast.

John Oxenham was lying near the rail, cursing in a peevish voice while he tugged at an arrow that was sunk into his side up to the very feathering.

The boarders had six swords, and the sixth swordsman was Harry Coppledick, a cousin of the bully whose shoulder Talbot had broken. But Harry had never even reached *Gillard's Pride*, for he had been killed by a musket ball while making the leap, and had fallen into the sea, sword and all.

The rest of *El Drague's* crew, armed only with clubs, and some of them not armed at all, did not dare to venture from behind the fighting screens.

"Well, we're four here," Captain Drake said. "Enough to take any ship, if God be with us, eh?"

He turned to Talbot, panting.

"What now, sir?"

Talbot did not answer immediately. He was studying the situation.

Four motionless mariners marked the path of these four swordsmen from rail to mainmast. There were ten or eleven others nearby, gripping pikes and cutlasses, screwing up their courage for a rush. Despite the odds, Talbot had considerable hope. These men were Channel pirates, great fellows for boarding but not so good in defense. To be attacked was a new sensation for them, and they did not like it.

Directly above were some archers; he couldn't look to see how many. At the moment these were not to be feared, for the four swordsmen from *El Draque* could not be reached by them, and were in fact marooned on a little island of safety—of temporary safety. The archers, in consequence, were shooting not down but at the figures behind the screens, to prevent further boarding.

Back on the poop, clearly visible despite the gathering darkness, was Thomas Gillard of Gillard's Elm. He had taken no part in the fighting so far—a circumstance which at the time puzzled Talbot, who knew what Tom Gillard, whatever else he might be, was no coward. Then Talbot saw Gillard's companions, and understood.

One was a tall, stiff Spaniard, who stared disdainfully, without any show of interest, at the fighting. The other was Ratface.

These were the men Talbot and Captain Drake had come to get, and Gillard knew it. Gillard would remain close to these men. As a last resort, if the battle went against him, he would make some excuse to kill them.

Talbot was convinced of this.

Gillard roared: "At them, ye goose-livered clods!"

The mariners charged again, before Talbot was able to reach a decision, and for a few minutes there was no time for anything but debate.

Ellis Hixom was brought to his knees. He leaned with one shoulder against the mast, moaning.

Talbot's left arm was cut twice again because he had forgotten for a moment that he no longer had any defense there and had exposed the arm by facing an antagonist squarely. But he still was laughing, and he felt incalculably strong.

He wished that he dared to look toward Katherine.

Above the shouts, the shuffling of feet, the grunts and curses and squeals of pain, the clang and scrape of steel, he could hear Tom Gillard roaring commands to cut loose the two vessels. Talbot could hear axes biting into the base of *El Draque*'s bow grapnel.

Conceivably Gillard's failure to join the fight had caused his men some discouragement. He would have to come down soon.

The shallop, *Gillard's Pride*, was tossing in rising seas, and in truth it was in a bad way. Tom Gillard's command to cut her loose from *El Draque* was more than a battle order. *El Draque*, being the heavier vessel, with a much greater spread of canvas, was able to ride with the wind, pushing the shallop ahead of her, so that *Gillard's Pride*, half turned, was taking the seas almost broadside. She was not built for such punishment.

Gillard's Pride never had been a handy vessel in dirty weather. Now she was slammed and battered unmercifully, and the man at her tiller was powerless to prevent this. She lurched free of the fregata when at last the grapnel was chopped through, but a heavy sea whirled her madly and all but stood her on end.

Talbot, together with most of the others, was thrown to the deck. He was scrambling to his feet, still clutching his rapier, when some instinct warned him to look aloft.

He yelled, and threw himself upon the deck again, covering his head with his arms.

The mainmast made a shrill, dry sound when it split, but it struck the deck like a crash of thunder. The shallop heaved wildly to starboard, and Talbot slid along the rough pine boards, scratching his face and hands, shredding his clothes.

He struck a rail, got to one knee, looked around.

The fighting tower, a rickety overcrowded structure at best, had been plunged into the sea, archers and all.

Tom Moone lay moaning, his face white with pain, an arm twisted underneath him.

Ellis Hixom was a crumpled heap against the stump of the mast: a splinter the size of a lance had been driven into his left shoulder.

The mast itself was gone, and so were at least five or six of the mariners who fought for Tom Gillard, while the others looked helpless, stunned.

Captain Drake, who could never cease to struggle, was on his knees, striving to regain his feet.

A hundred yards away, untouched by the fallen mast, floated the fregata *El Draque*.

Talbot ran for the poop. He had seen Tom Gillard draw his dagger, and he knew what Gillard was about to do.

Nobody made any attempt to stop Talbot. The mari-

185

ners were confused, shaken, badly frightened, without a leader to rally them. They had had enough of fighting.

Tom Gillard's left arm went up. It looked, from where Talbot Slanning was running, as though Gillard had given the tall Spaniard a hearty slap between the shoulder blades. The Spaniard, still stiff, unyielding, pitched forward on his face. A lurch of the vessel rolled him into the scuppers.

Gillard wheeled upon Ratface, who shrank away.

Talbot yelled: "Stop! You will live!"

Either Ratface did not understand the English or he was too badly scared to hear anything at all—or to know anything, except that Captain Gillard was about to kill him. He was staring at Gillard as though fascinated, a rabbit before a snake. But he did succeed in stumbling backward, and he struck the rail.

Talbot, running, yelled: "Come this way!"

Gillard leaped. Ratface, screeching, scrambled over the rail and fell into the sea.

Captain Drake ran past Talbot.

"We must have that man!"

Drake dropped his sword and helmet and dived head-first over the rail, which his body never touched.

Then Talbot confronted Tom Gillard.

Gillard smiled slowly, and slowly he nodded.

"You come too late, messenger boy."

Talbot said: "Not too late to kill you."

The light was poor. The poop rose and fell as the shallop, out of all control, pitched wildly, and seas ankle-deep sloshed across *Gillard's Pride*. However, the poop was comparatively free of tackle and rope coils and wreckage from the smashed cabin. And nobody disturbed them as they fought. For all they themselves knew, or cared, they might have been the only two men in the world.

They did not really hear the crackling of timbers. They knew that the shallop was afire; for presently their figures glowed red in the failing light, and their blades shone in the fiery light like stiffened strips of flame; but this too they did not mind.

The cresset from which the archers had ignited their fire-arrows had fallen directly upon the wreckage of the cabin, which still was dry then. *Gillard's Pride* blazed eagerly, almost gleefully, as though she had long awaited this chance to quit the world.

Talbot cried: "For William Abergavenny!"

He went in low, turning his wrist, cutting up. The end of his blade slipped soundlessly, effortlessly up Tom Gillard's right cheek, removing a goodly portion of the ear.

Gillard did not even seem to be aware of this. He too was glad to fight, and he was utterly silent, utterly savage. He played for Talbot's left flank, for he had seen that Talbot's left arm was useless.

Talbot stood with his right foot far forward, his right shoulder advanced. He made no crosses and no side steps.

He cried: "For Robert Butterwalk, murderer!"

Abruptly the left side of Gillard's face was opened from chin to ear. Blood splattered over his doublet and hose, yet he did not pause.

The sun was setting, unnoticed, ignored. It made the sea an angry sullen red, the sky a smoky darker crimson. But this was a dying light, a far light. The glare of the blaze aboard *Gillard's Pride* was much more immediate, more real, livelier: the flames crackled and spat in malicious glee, and threw a restless giddy scarlet upon the evening air.

Talbot began to laugh. He was not hysterical. He knew that he was the better swordsman, and that in spite of the heaving deck, the wet boards, the uncertain light,

in spite also of his wounded left arm, he would kill
Thomas Gillard very soon.

Gillard knew it too. Talbot could read this in his eyes.

"The next one will be for me," Talbot told him.

Gillard dropped into a deep lunge, thrusting straight.
It was the last desperate trick of a gambler. Until now
he had been plying the edge only, but he was turning
Talbot's own technique against him. It was a starkly
simple attack, very swift, unexpected.

It almost succeeded. Talbot caught the blade barely
in time, lifting it, and he felt it slither along his own
sword as he straightened his right arm.

Tom Gillard fell without a sound, but with such force
that the sword was wrenched out of Talbot's grip and
slammed upon the deck underneath Gillard. Above, glittering in the mad little scarlet lights of the fire, the sword
stuck a full five inches out of Tom Gillard's back. It must
have gone directly through Gillard's heart.

Talbot was not laughing now. He felt weak, and a
little sick. He felt a little frightened too, for the first
time. He sat down with his back against the foremast,
and held his head in his hands. A pitch of the vessel
threw him sideways, and rolled him into the scuppers,
and he found himself all but kneeling upon the figure of
the tall Spaniard who had been stabbed in the back. A
corpse coming to life? Talbot gasped. For the eyes were
open and wildly staring, and the lips moved.

Talbot rose, yelling in his excitement.

"He's alive! He's still alive!"

From the starboard rail a few feet away came Francis
Drake's voice: "So is this one."

The Captain's head appeared. He was panting,
coughing, laboring to drag something after him as he
struggled out of the water and over the rail. Talbot ran
to his help.

"Aye, this one too."

Ratface was very wet, thoroughly frightened, and breathless; but decidedly he was alive. They hauled him over the rail, threw him upon the deck.

All fight had gone out of the mariners of *Gillard's Pride*. They were crowded in the bow, throwing their weapons into the sea, frantically waving and shouting to those of the fregata to come and take them off.

Gillard's Pride was sinking.

El Draque moved in cautiously until her crippled grapnel-arm ground against the bow of the shallop. Talbot could see Katherine Abergavenny on the half-deck, waving both her arms.

The men were throwing grappling hooks and nets, this time without resistance, and the mariners of *Gillard's Pride* scrambled eagerly to safety.

There was a mass of roaring flames between that safety and the poop deck of the shallop. Francis Drake tore long strips from his own wet doublet, and with these he and Talbot swabbed the faces of the two Spaniards. Talbot took the tall Spaniard over his shoulder. Drake took Ratface.

The corpse of Thomas Gillard showed red in the light of the flames, with the end of Talbot's rapier still sticking out of its back.

The tall Spaniard, whose name was Jesus-Maria de Bazan, died—but not before he had first mumbled a confession of the whole assassination plot, which was witnessed not only by the principal officers and gentlemen of *El Draque* but also by the high sheriff of Devonshire, his deputies, and two Queen's commissioners.

Ratface likewise had confessed, without the slightest press. And his confession too was well and properly witnessed and recorded.

"And now," said Francis Drake, "it might be seemly if

189

we went to our knees and offered up a prayer to Almighty God, by Whose grace we have won through these perils."

"Amen," everybody said.

Talbot Slanning knelt by the side of Katherine, very close to her, and kept his eyes open while the Captain prayed. He watched the last far flickers of light that came across the deck from the place where the shallop, *Gillard's Pride*, was burning itself out in a last hissing spasm—its owner's funeral pyre, soon to disappear beneath the sea.

"I'll grant you success, Frank," the high sheriff grunted as he rose. "But it was a mighty wager to place upon one roll of the dice."

"I do not believe in gambling. It's a sin."

"But you'll win a pardon, aye."

"A pardon? Nay! I'll win more than that! I'll win the Queen's gracious permission to sail another sea. For this treasure's a trifle that lies beneath us now, eh, Slanning? The greatest treasure is yet to be won."

Talbot had his arm around Katherine Abergavenny. He smiled.

"The greatest treasure, for me," he said, "is won already."